TAKE A CHANCE

When Tessa unexpectedly loses her job, she tries to console herself by impulsively going on holiday to Spain, hoping that a sun-soaked restful break will help her face the future. But instead she finds herself involved in the affairs of Tom, an Englishman who has settled in the country, and two children who have apparently been abandoned by their father. She does her best to help them all, but will Tom's past stop her from finding happiness?

SHEILA HOLROYD

TAKE A
CHANCE

Complete and Unabridged

LINFORD
Leicester

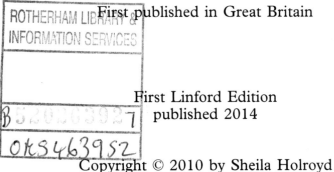

First published in Great Britain

First Linford Edition
published 2014

A catalogue record for this book is available
from the British Library.

ISBN 978–1–4448–1972–4

Published by
F. A. Thorpe (Publishing)
Anstey, Leicestershire

Set by Words & Graphics Ltd.
Anstey, Leicestershire
Printed and bound in Great Britain by
T. J. International Ltd., Padstow, Cornwall

This book is printed on acid-free paper

1

It had started as a normal, boring working day. Tessa had arrived at work punctually as usual, and had been working steadily through routine tasks until Mr Briggs, the manager, had opened his office door and called her in. Five minutes later she was staring at him in horror.

'You're sacking me?'

Tessa's voice was shrill with horror and Mr Briggs, seated safely behind the wide expanse of his desk, shook his head urgently.

'No, my dear. I'm making you redundant, and that's a very different thing. You know the business has not been doing well in these hard times, and we just don't need so many office staff and, frankly, we can't afford to pay you all. Of course, you'll get an excellent reference,' Mr Briggs continued soothingly.

'I'll write it myself. I'll be sorry to say goodbye to you at the end of the week, Miss Saunders.'

'You mean this Friday? So soon?'

'I'm afraid so. The sooner the better for the firm, as I'm sure you'll appreciate. Now, if you'll just send in Miss Thomson . . . '

He clasped his hands on his large stomach and waited for her to obey. For a moment she stared at him, seething with fury but unable to find the words to express her anger and hurt. She turned, fumbled to open the door and emerged into the outer office, blinking away tears. Her friend and co-worker, Diane Thomson, looked at her enquiringly and then pushed back her chair and started to rise.

'Are you all right, Tessa? You look very pale. Has Mr Briggs upset you?'

Tessa hurriedly dabbed at her eyes and tried to smile.

'I'll tell you all about it later. Mr Briggs wants to see you now.'

As her friend went into the inner

office Tessa sank down at her desk and held her head in her hands. She had to acknowledge that business had not been good recently for the firm, which imported wines and sold them to shops and hotels, but she had worked there since she left school at eighteen, four years ago, and had always thought of herself as an asset to the firm, a hard worker who never refused a task and was willing to work unpaid overtime when necessary, and she could hardly believe that she was now considered dispensable, surplus to requirements. And at such short notice! In less than a week she would be out of work, expelled from these familiar surroundings for ever.

She was shocked into awareness a few minutes later when Mr Briggs' office door was opened and then slammed shut so vigorously that it shook and it looked as if the frosted panel of glass would break. Diane's face was flushed, her teeth bared in an angry scowl as she stalked through the office.

'Oh no, not you as well?' Tessa exclaimed, and Diane nodded curtly.

'Apparently neither of us is needed after this week,' she said loudly. 'Miss Carter is going to do all the office work by herself. Did you know you were going to do that, Miss Carter?'

She was standing, hands on hips, addressing Mr Briggs' secretary, a timid middle-aged lady who had been trying to pretend that she was engrossed by the figures on her computer, a machine which she feared and had great difficulty in using. Miss Carter hesitated, and then nodded reluctantly.

'Then why didn't you warn us?' Diane almost shouted, and Miss Carter looked on the edge of tears.

'Mr Briggs made me promise not to,' she quavered, fishing up the sleeve of her ancient cardigan for her handkerchief, dabbing at her eyes and then blowing her nose vigorously.

There was no point in reproaching her. Tessa and Diane were both in their early twenties and would probably not have too much difficulty finding new jobs, but if Miss Carter had been made redundant it would have been almost impossible for her to find another post, a fact of which Mr Briggs was well aware and of which he took full advantage.

'Well, if he's expecting you to do the work of three people, make sure you ask him for a rise,' Diane snapped.

Miss Carter looked at her dolefully, twisting the handkerchief in her fingers.

'Mr Briggs says he's not sure the firm can go on paying what I get now, that he might have to cut my salary.'

Diane sat down by the older woman, her own situation temporarily forgotten, and took her hand.

'Well, that's nonsense. If he cut down on his long business lunches he'd have plenty of time to run the firm properly and more spare cash to pay for you. And don't forget, he'll have our wages to play with now he's getting rid of the two of us. Don't let him keep the lot. Just imagine what a hopeless mess he'd be in if all his office staff left at once and point that out to him.'

Tessa went to the cloakroom, where she wiped away the signs of tears from her hazel eyes and combed her shoulder-length light-brown hair. She gazed miserably at the face in the mirror — unwanted, unemployed. Then she squared her shoulders and lifted her chin. Life would go on.

A little work did get done that afternoon while Mr Briggs remained hidden in his office, but both Tessa and Diane stopped work at exactly five o'clock that afternoon as a minor act of defiance, even though a few small tasks remained unfinished.

'In a way I'll be glad to leave this place,' Diane confided as they put their coats on. 'It's been a steady job, but it's been dull, and I've never liked Mr Briggs. At least now I can look for something more interesting.'

'We'll talk about it at lunchtime tomorrow,' Tessa promised.

When Tessa got home that evening

her mother was in the kitchen preparing the evening meal.

'Hello, Tessa. Had a good day?' she called out.

This was her invariable greeting.

'No,' Tessa said bitterly. 'I've lost my job. I've been sacked.'

There was the sound of a plate breaking as it hit the floor and her mother appeared in the kitchen doorway, eyes wide with shock.

'You've lost your job? What did you do?'

'Nothing!' said Tessa indignantly. She had been expecting sympathy. 'Mr Briggs has let the firm run down and now he can't afford to pay me or Diane.'

Her father arrived home soon afterwards and she told her parents the whole story but was disappointed by their reactions. She had expected horror and anger on her behalf, something to match her own tumult of feelings. But her mother, who spent a lot of her time playing bridge or at coffee-mornings, had never worked for her living and tended to see Tessa's job as something which would keep her occupied until she got married and started on her real career, which would be to provide a steady supply of grandchildren. Her father was a little more aware of how upset Tessa was, but did not see it as a serious matter or realise quite how demoralised she felt.

'It's been useful experience for you,' he said philosophically, 'but you've been there long enough. A change will probably do you good. And don't worry,' he assured her. 'We'll support you until you get another job.'

It was true that the small contribution which Tessa had insisted on making to the family finances was not important to them, though it had been good for Tessa's self-esteem, but she was aware that the loss of income would matter to Diane, who didn't have the advantage of a family to support her and who had to pay the rent on her bed-sit.

Tessa was reluctant to get up and go to work the next day. She usually got out of bed as soon as the alarm went off, but now she snuggled down for an extra ten minutes. If she wouldn't be needed in a few days' time, then she wasn't needed now, so why should she bother? A sense of duty finally made her fling back the bedclothes and make for the bathroom, so that she was ready to leave the house at nearly the normal time. Miss Carter, as usual, had got to the office first, but to Tessa's surprise Diane had also arrived early and was sitting in front of her computer, tapping away with face flushed and eyes sparkling militantly, a pile of print-outs by her side.

'As soon as Mr Briggs arrives, I've got something to discuss with him, and he isn't going to be happy,' she announced.

'What about? Anything I should know?'

'Well, I went out to a club last night to cheer myself up. I told some friends what had happened and they gave me some very interesting information. I've just been checking up on what they said . . . '

But at this moment the door opened and Mr Briggs swept in. His only greeting to the two girls was a brief nod as he proceeded to his private office.

'I'll give him five minutes to take his coat off and settle down,' murmured Diane.

'He'll be expecting me to take him his morning coffee first of all,' Miss Carter reminded her, picking up the office kettle.

'He can wait for it for once,' Diane informed her so firmly that Miss Carter abandoned the kettle and sat down.

Five minutes went by, and then Diane stood up, picked up the print-outs, took a deep breath, knocked sharply on Mr Briggs' door and went in without waiting for a response. Twenty minutes passed. Occasionally a raised voice could be heard. Miss Carter and Tessa abandoned any attempt to work and sat watching the door, Miss Carter wincing at any particularly loud exchange. Finally the door opened as Diane strode out and banged it behind her, and then she marched over to Tessa's desk and slapped a slip of paper down in front to her.

'Yours,' she said triumphantly.

Tessa picked it up and stared at it. Her eyes widened and she looked up at Diane in total bewilderment. It was a cheque for four hundred pounds, made out to Tessa Saunders and duly signed by Mr Briggs. Tessa examined it again in disbelief. Her employer was not known for his generosity.

'What's this for?' she managed to ask.

'It's your redundancy money. I've got the same. I pointed out to our Mr Briggs that as we have both worked for this firm for more than two years we were entitled to redundancy compensation. He tried to argue, but I showed him what the Government web-site said. I also mentioned that we should have been given adequate notice.' She pursed her lips thoughtfully. 'Perhaps we should have got a few pounds more, but at least I got this much out of him, though I think we'd better get the cheques paid in before he tries to cancel them. I don't trust him.'

Miss Carter was clapping her hands.

'Good for you, Diane!' she said.

Clearly even she was developing a spirit of rebellion. Tessa wondered what the coming weeks would be like in the office. Well, it wouldn't be her concern.

A little work did get done that morning, though not much. Mr Briggs, who once again had stayed hidden in his office, appeared just before lunch-time and announced that he would not be back for the rest of the day. Neither Tessa nor Diane had brought their usual packed lunches, and instead they took themselves off to a nearby café. Tessa bought a copy of the local paper on the way and once they had ordered she began to comb the Situations Vacant columns, putting the paper down when their food arrived.

'There aren't many secretarial jobs,' she sighed. 'Do you want to look?'

Diane shook her head emphatically.

'No.' She put down her knife and fork and looked at Tessa with resolution. 'Tessa, we've both spent years doing basically boring jobs for Briggs, and I don't want to go straight into another. I think we deserve a break.'

Tessa sat up.

'You mean a weekend away? That might be fun. How about a couple of days in London? We could book tickets for that new musical.'

But Diane was shaking her head again.

'Not a weekend. I think we should spend our redundancy money on a proper holiday. I was thinking of somewhere abroad — somewhere sunny.'

Tessa's fork clattered to her plate.

'Diane! That money is to help tide us over till we get other jobs. We can't waste it all on a holiday.'

'It wouldn't be wasted! We need something to cheer us up and give us the energy to start deciding what to do with the rest of our lives. You know your parents will support you if you don't get a job straightaway, and I . . . '

'You need to pay the rent!'

'Okay, but I've got enough saved up to survive for a few weeks.' She leant forward, her voice becoming soft and persuasive. 'Listen to me, Tessa. We could get new jobs straight away, in which case we won't need the redundancy money to keep us going. And if we don't get jobs and find ourselves facing a dark and dismal future, then I think we should have the memory of something enjoyable to look back on — like sun, sea, and sand.' She waved a hand at the window, where the chilly February rain was beating down.

But cautious Tessa was not to be persuaded, though even she was momentarily tempted by the vision of a carefree holiday with Diane.

'It would be an unjustified waste of money,' she said virtuously.

'At least think about it,' her friend

14

urged. 'It will be a lot cheaper if there are two of us sharing a room.'

That evening Tessa had her usual weekly dinner date with Eric Lester. She had been going out with Eric for some time now, long enough for her mother to talk about them hopefully as 'going steady'. He was an assistant bank manager, a serious young man who intended to do well in his career, and Tessa's mother thought him the ideal partner for her daughter. Tessa was undecided.

They met at the Chinese restaurant where they usually ate. It was family-owned and they were greeted cheerfully by the owner and then his elder daughter, attractive and very efficient, bustled up to take their order — or rather to confirm their order.

'Will it be the usual?' she said brightly. 'Seaweed for you, madam, and soup for the gentleman, then Tibetan lamb and Chinese beef, with one egg-fried rice, and two glasses of house red?'

Eric nodded, and Tessa felt a brief spurt of annoyance. He might have asked her if that was what she wanted first, not just taken her agreement for granted. Like so much of her life, dinner with Eric had settled into a repetitive routine.

'I think I'll have spring rolls as a starter for a change,' she announced, and saw a flash of amusement on the Chinese girl's face. Had she guessed what Tessa was feeling?

At least tonight, instead of listening to Eric talk about his activities at the bank, she could break the news of how badly she had been treated and complain bitterly about her employer. As soon as the first course had arrived she launched into her story.

'So Mr Briggs decided that Diane and I are no longer necessary. I know the firm hasn't been doing well but that's largely his fault. He can't be bothered to make the effort to find new customers and spends half his time having long expense-account lunches with his cronies.'

Eric tut-tutted sadly, but then frowned.

'So you're going to be unemployed. It's a bad time to lose your job and being made redundant won't look good on your CV. Employers tend to think you would have been kept on if you'd been any good.'

'Thank you very much,' Tessa said coldly, glaring at him, but he was too busy spooning up the last of his soup to notice. So much for the sympathy she had expected! The rest of the meal passed in virtual silence, though that was not uncommon. They had few mutual interests to talk about.

They had always divided the cost of their meals equally between them, with Eric paying for any drinks. Tessa had insisted on this from the first because it made her feel like an equal and not under any obligation to be nice to him in return for the price of a meal. She knew that he earned a lot more than she did and sometimes thought he could offer to pay a larger share, even though she also knew that he was very careful with money, or, as he preferred to put it, prudent. However, she did feel that tonight, in view of the fact that she had lost her job and therefore her income, he might offer to treat her. Instead he checked the bill carefully, as always, added the minimum acceptable tip, divided the total by half, and waited for her to hand him her share. She made a great show of having to hunt through her bag to find the necessary amount and counted it out to him very ostentatiously, but he didn't seem to notice.

At least he drove her home, though he refused her polite invitation to come in for coffee on the grounds that he had an important meeting the next morning and wanted to go over some papers before he went to bed.

'Goodnight, Tessa. See you next week,' he said, bending forward to kiss her on the cheek. He never tried to make any more daring amorous advances. Tessa told herself that he was showing her respect, but sometimes had to admit that she was relieved by his restrained behaviour. In spite of his obvious virtues he did not particularly attract her and she did not want him to show any more ardour. As she felt in her bag for her key while watching his car drive away, she wondered why she continued going out with him if she didn't really feel much liking for him. She had to be honest with herself and admit that perhaps she only went on seeing him because she hadn't met anyone better and didn't like to feel completely unwanted. It was a very depressing thought.

Back at the office the next morning, both Tessa and Diane resumed the task of finishing off any outstanding work. They were definitely not doing this for Mr Briggs' benefit, but so that life would not be too difficult for Miss Carter when they were gone. They were fond of the older woman and were sure that she would have a hard time coping when they had left.

'She won't be able to manage by

herself,' Diane had said. 'Just think of her having to deal with all the internet communications! In a fortnight's time everything will be in a complete mess. Oh well, at least Mr Briggs won't be able to blame us.'

Mr Briggs had claimed he would be visiting clients all day, and half-way through the morning Tessa noticed that Diane seemed to be showing more interest in what her computer was displaying than a few documents on wine-selling deserved. Finding an excuse to pass behind Diane, she saw a message blazoned across the screen — 'Holiday Prices Slashed!'

'Diane, we're not supposed to use the computers for our private affairs,' she said uneasily, but Diane waved her to silence.

'Wait a minute! I think I've found just what we want.' She tapped away for a minute, and then clicked on an arrow, before raising her hands above her head in triumph. 'Yes! Two weeks in southern Spain, full-board at a four-star hotel. We can afford it if we share a room.'

'I've told you I'm not going!' Tessa stated as firmly as she could.

Diane swung her chair round and looked at her with entreaty in her eyes.

'We must! We need a break before we start job-hunting! If you won't go I can't afford to go on my own.'

Before they could say any more Miss Carter was at the desk, looking agitated.

'Girls! You're making a lot of noise.'

'It doesn't matter. Sir isn't here.'

Miss Carter continued to hover.

'Do you want something?' Diane enquired impatiently, eager to resume her attempts to persuade Tessa to come on holiday.

Miss Carter swallowed nervously.

'I just wanted to ask you to make sure that your desks are clear when you leave on Friday, so that the new man doesn't have to sort anything out.'

Tessa and Diane stared at her blankly.

'The new man? But the firm is cutting down on staff. That's why we're leaving.' Diane's face showed dawning indignation. 'Don't tell me Mr Briggs is getting rid of us but taking on another employee! Who is it? A salesman to do the work he's supposed to do?'

Miss Carter fidgeted uneasily.

'Not exactly a salesman — Mr Briggs said he would be a 'factotum', whatever that is.'

'A dogsbody — someone who does any old job that needs doing,' Tessa said. 'Do you know anything about him? Is it some sixteen-year old who'll be paid peanuts and who doesn't realise what a miserable time he's going to have?'

Miss Carter shook her head and swallowed nervously, doing her best to avoid looking at them directly.

'No. In fact, I think you've seen him once or twice when he's called in.' She hesitated. 'It's Mr Briggs' nephew,' she finished in a rush.

There was a stunned silence, broken by Tessa.

'Do you mean that spotty, repulsive,

conceited youth, the one with the wandering hands? I nearly slapped his face the last time he was here.'

Miss Carter gave a miserable nod, and Tessa turned to her friend. Indignant fury was sweeping away all thoughts of prudence.

'Diane — book that holiday — now!'

Diane's hands raced over the keyboard.

'Booked!' she said triumphantly.

Tessa collapsed on a chair. Her legs suddenly felt weak as she realised what they'd done.

'So we're going to Spain for two weeks?'

Diane nodded cheerfully.

'Full-board and a four-star hotel?'

Diane nodded again.

Tessa swallowed.

'When do we leave?'

'Tomorrow morning at nine o'clock.'

It took a few seconds for this to sink in, and then Tessa sat up abruptly.

'What?' she squealed.

'Tomorrow at nine o'clock,' Diane repeated slowly and clearly, as if her friend had suddenly gone deaf.

Tessa's eyes widened in panic and she waved her hands frantically.

'But we can't! We're working here till Friday afternoon. Cancel it!'

Diane folded her hands firmly in her lap and shook her head.

'We'll take time off in lieu of the holiday we are owed.'

They were surprised by a strange cackling noise. It was the rare sound of Miss Carter's laughter.

'Go and enjoy yourselves, girls. I'll take great pleasure in telling Mr Briggs why you aren't coming in. I think he's treated you both very badly.'

Diane stood up and gave the older woman a dazzling smile.

'You do that, Miss Carter. He won't dare say anything to you because he knows he'd never be able to manage without you. Come on, Tessa. Say goodbye to this place. We're leaving now. We've got things to do before tomorrow morning.'

It was strange to walk out of the

familiar office, knowing it was for the very last time and leaving uncompleted tasks on their desks. Tessa glanced back at the small stuffy room with the dismal brown paintwork and the battered desks. She realised she would not miss it at all and her heart lightened. She waved goodbye to Miss Carter and turned her back on the place where she had spent four long years without another look.

'I should have tried to find another job ages ago,' she fretted. 'I only stayed there because it seemed so safe and secure — and look how wrong I was.'

'Maybe we'll end up thanking Mr Briggs for making us redundant,' Diane said cheerfully. 'Anyway, I'll see you at the check-in desk for the Malaga flight at a quarter to seven tomorrow morning. Don't forget your passport!'

Her mother didn't bother to ask how her day had been.

'It must have been sad,' she commiserated. 'You've been there so long, and now suddenly you've only got a couple of days more to spend there.'

'Not even a couple of days. I'm never going back there again,' Tessa told her airily, 'Diane and I are going to Spain in the morning.'

For a moment she was afraid her mother was going to break another plate.

Tessa's latest news was greeted by both parents with more surprise than the news of her redundancy had been.

'You have to plan holidays. You can't just go off at a moment's notice,' her mother protested after her daughter had given her the full details.

'Yes I can. All I have to do is pack a few clothes and turn up at the airport.'

'And how do you intend to do that?' her father asked resignedly, and she looked at him beseechingly.

'I thought — as this is to console me for losing my job — that you might help by driving me there.'

'In the middle of the night?' he scoffed, but then grinned. 'Of course I will, my love. Just be careful. This will be your first holiday without us, so don't go falling for some handsome Spaniard.'

Her mother groaned. Another threat to her daughter!

Tessa found her summer clothes at the back of her wardrobe, added a swimming costume, then a towel. The pile looked very small. She began to add extra garments, such as a couple of jumpers, just in case the weather turned cold. Then she thought she might need something dressy for the evenings and added a few more things. By the time she had finished the pile had grown enormous and she had to go through it, weeding out the more unnecessary items, until finally her suitcase was comfortably full. All the time she was regretting the impulse which had put her in this position. She and Diane had got along fairly well working together, partly because of their mutual dislike for Mr Briggs, but how would they get along in close proximity for a fortnight in Spain?

She realised at one point that she hadn't let Eric Lester know what she was doing. Unless she called him he would turn up at the Chinese restaurant in a week's time and sit there vainly waiting for her to join him. Her hand hovered over the telephone and then she moved away. Let him wait and let him fret. She didn't care if she never saw him again. She found she was enjoying the novelty of behaving badly.

Both Tessa's parents were waiting for her when she went downstairs next morning when the alarm clock sounded after only a few hours of uneasy sleep. She was too nervous to eat the large breakfast her mother cooked for her, and soon she was kissing her goodbye and promising to take care of herself and avoid all the temptations that a holiday in Spain might bring. Her father said nothing until they reached the airport. As he took her suitcase out of the car boot, he suddenly chuckled.

'You know, Tessa, you've always been such a good, quiet girl. I think this is the first time you've surprised me. I'm waiting to see what you'll do next. Here.' He took some bank notes out of his pocket and thrust them towards her. 'You'll need some spending money. Enjoy yourself.'

She took the notes gratefully and then threw her arms round him impulsively.

'Thanks, Dad, and I will!'

She watched him drive away and then pulled her suitcase into the half-empty departure hall and looked round for Diane. Her friend stood near the door, looking strained and anxious. When Tessa called her she spun round and her face lightened.

'So you came!'

'Did you think I might not come?'

Diane swallowed.

'Well, I woke up in the middle of the night and decided that we were being complete fools.'

'So we are, but we're going to enjoy being foolish. Anyway, we can't cancel now or we'll lose all our money as well as missing out on our holiday.'

'We could claim it back from the insurance company on the grounds of temporary insanity.'

There was a hint of hysteria in their laughter. Tessa picked up her luggage again.

'Now, what do we do?'

'We check in.'

'What does that involve?'

Diane looked at her with surprise.

'Haven't you flown before?'

'No, so show me what to do.'

Checking-in and getting rid of their baggage did not take long and then they went through to the departure lounge. Diane sank down and stared at her friend.

'Tessa, how have you avoided flying in this day and age?'

'I've always gone on holiday with my parents to somewhere in England. Mother didn't want to go anywhere where they didn't speak English, and my father likes visiting castles and great houses, so we spent our holidays visiting National Trust properties.'

'So why did you get a passport?'

'I went on a school trip to France. We crossed the Channel by ferry and spent three days visiting museums in Paris.'

Diane laughed, her face lighting up gleefully.

'I think you'll find this holiday is very different!'

Then there was nothing to do but sit and wait till it was time to board their plane. They were silent most of the time, both secretly wondering if they should still do the sensible thing and walk out of the airport and spend the next few days job-hunting instead of sunbathing. But neither voiced their misgivings to the other, so when the flight was announced they both boarded the plane and took their seats. Tessa held her breath as the plane sped along the runway and felt dizzy when she looked down and saw they had risen above the fields and villages. She spent a lot of the flight gazing out of the window and noted grimly that the cloud cover was unbroken over Spain.

'What are you thinking?' Diane asked at one point.

'I'm trying to remember why aeroplanes stay up in the sky.'

She saw some of the nearby passengers who had overheard her stare at her and said nothing more for the rest of the flight. She gave a great gasp of relief when the plane finally touched down and came to a halt.

The travel rep collected them at Malaga together with half-a-dozen other clients, and while they were being driven to their hotel all they could see was a wet and dismal landscape as heavy rain lashed the sides of their coach. Obviously this was a sign that the heavens were punishing them for their imprudence.

They were the only two to be dropped off at their hotel, and when they reached it they grabbed their bags from the minibus and dashed through the main doors in search of shelter. After five minutes at the reception desk they were given the keys to their hotel room. It was pleasant enough. It was quite large and had a balcony with a view of the grey, wave-flecked sea, and Tessa welcomed it as sanctuary after the hours of travel and her first experience of flying.

'What do we do now?' she asked weakly.

Diane was unzipping her case.

'We unpack, and then we have a sleep — a siesta, as we're in Spain. We're both too tired to think properly now.' She stepped away from her case. 'In fact, the unpacking can wait. We need to sleep.'

So that was what they did, scrambling out of the warm skirts and jumpers that February in England had required and collapsing on the beds.

Tessa woke with a jerk and looked round the unfamiliar room, remembering where she was only when she saw Diane snoring gently in the other bed. There was a rosy glow outside the window and she swung herself off her bed and padded over to investigate. Opening the glass door and slipping out on to the balcony, she found herself gazing at a scene which had undergone a miraculous transformation. The red ball of the sun was just setting in a cloudless sky, turning everything rosy-gold, silhouetting tree-topped cliffs and illuminating the calm sea. Tessa heard Diane move behind her and then her friend's sharp intake of breath. She laughed.

'We did the right thing, Diane. We're going to have a wonderful holiday.'

2

Filled with new energy, they unpacked, hanging up their clothes and assuring each other that the creases would drop out. Tessa was pleased to discover that there was a safe in the wardrobe where they could store their passports and travel documents as well as money and credit cards and other valuable items. It gave her some sense of security in this strange land.

Diane showered first and then Tessa took her turn and came out to find that Diane had put on a light, full-skirted dress which she had not worn since the previous summer. She twirled round, finishing with a curtsey to her friend.

'Look! Isn't it marvellous to be able to wear something like this in February? In fact, come to think of it, I didn't get many chances to wear it last summer in England.'

She was looking at her watch as Tessa brushed her tousled hair after choosing her own dress, one of which her mother disapproved because she thought the neckline too revealing.

'Dinner started ten minutes ago and I'm hungry. Shall we go down and meet the other guests?' Diane grinned wickedly. 'And before we do that, before we find out how many attractive men we have to choose from, let me tell you how I treat holiday romances. They're great fun, very enjoyable, but they are just for the holiday. I don't want to see my sun-tanned hero once the holiday is over. Understood?'

Tessa shrugged.

'You forget, I've never been on holiday without my parents so I've never had a holiday romance.'

Diane sighed and gazed at her solemnly.

'Do you mean all your boyfriends have been the serious, respectable type like your banker whatshisname? At your age, that's very sad and you've missed out on a lot. It's high time you found out what fun a short holiday romance with some irresponsible charmer can be. We'll definitely have to see if we can find you a suitable partner for the next two weeks.'

Tessa shook her head.

'It doesn't sound my type of thing, Diane. Anyway, I promised my mother I'd behave. I'm going to swim, sunbathe and sightsee, and possibly learn a little about Spanish culture.'

Diane looked at her sceptically.

'If you say so, but you can always change your mind, and you know you don't have to tell your mother everything.'

Tessa made a disapproving face, and then picked up a silver and amethyst necklace.

'Shall I wear this? I suppose I shouldn't have brought it on holiday because it is quite valuable, but it does go with this dress.'

'Wear it,' urged her friend. 'What's the use of pretty things if they're not seen? Anyway, you can put it in the room safe afterwards.'

Tessa fastened the clasp round her throat, admired the final effect in the mirror, and then they found their way down to the restaurant, which was already busy. Hesitating at the door, one swift look told them the awful truth that romantic partners would be hard to find. Apart from a few shiny bald pates, the predominant hair colour was grey.

'It's for oldies!' Diane groaned softly, and then managed a very artificial smile as the maitre d'hotel greeted them.

'You have just arrived?' he checked. 'Then let me put you with some guests who will be able to tell you all about the hotel and the area around it.'

He led them to a table whose tenants clearly had an average age of at least seventy. They were eager to welcome the young newcomers, however, and to chat with them, and it turned out that most of them were there for several weeks.

'No shopping, no cooking, no house-work — and sun most of the time,' one said cheerfully. 'There are advantages to being old and retired.'

'And there's so much to do! Do you play bridge?' one woman asked.

Her large husband smiled.

'Two young girls like these will have more interesting things to do than play cards.'

This earned a reproving glare from his wife.

'But what are you two doing here?' one inquisitive diner asked. 'You're certainly not retired!'

Diane smiled sweetly.

'We had an unexpected windfall and decided to use it to have an early holiday.'

'Probably won something on the lottery or bingo,' Tessa heard the woman who had asked about bridge mutter. She was momentarily offended. Did she look like a gambler?

At least the food was good and their companions were full of information about the hotel and the neighbourhood. Apparently the fertile land near the sea was mostly planted with orchards of fruit such as avocados, oranges and grapefruit, and behind them rose an impressive range of hills, with the Sierra Nevada mountain range behind them.

'It's beautiful round here,' they were assured repeatedly. Tessa, who had remembered to bring her camera, began to think that at least she should get some good pictures out of the holiday, something to show her parents.

The girls stopped at the door of the lounge after dinner, wondering where they should sit. Armchairs were already being formed into small groups and they did not want to trespass on anybody's accustomed seat. A woman elegantly dressed in red saw their hesitation and was quick to calm their fears.

'It's all right. You can sit where you like. There are plenty of spare seats but if you want to sit with other people most of them will welcome strangers, especially pretty young girls.'

Reassured, they politely refused various invitations to join groups and instead chose to sit down a little apart from the rest and ordered coffee.

'It will be easier to slip out if we're by ourselves, and we'll probably feel like an early night,' murmured Diane, and Tessa agreed. However, after the activities of the past twenty-four hours it was very pleasant to relax for a while in comfortable armchairs and listen to a pianist playing melodies from decades ago.

'To think that a few hours ago we were sure we had made a big mistake,' murmured Diane. 'Now look at us. After a good meal we are sitting here relaxing, with nothing to do and nothing to worry about.'

But there was an interruption. Without asking them for permission, a young man pulled a chair up and sat down next to them. He was in his mid twenties, with dark, flashy good looks and an air of self-confidence, his shirt-pocket embroidered with the name of a famous and expensive fashion designer.

'I'm glad to see you two good-looking girls have arrived,' he announced with a strong Spanish accent. 'I was getting bored here.' He added, a little late, 'Do you mind if I sit here?' The question was obviously a formality as far as he was concerned and he didn't wait for an answer. He clearly expected them to welcome him with delight and gratitude. Tessa disliked him on sight and wondered how they could get rid of him, but her friend was equal to the occasion.

'Certainly not,' was Diane's response as she smiled sweetly. 'We will move somewhere else.'

And she stood, picked up her coffee cup, and walked away rapidly to another empty set of chairs, followed by Tessa. The young man gazed after them in astonishment, an ugly flush of embarrassment rising in his cheeks as he heard the suppressed laughter from other guests who had witnessed the little scene.

'What a conceited idiot! Perhaps we'll be left alone now,' Diane commented.

But after a few minutes there was another interruption.

They heard a polite cough, obviously meant to attract their attention, and then, 'May I join you?' said a masculine voice. 'Of course, I'll understand if you don't want to be disturbed.'

Tessa looked up, scowling, prepared to rebuff the intruder, but instead both girls found themselves staring approvingly at the man who was waiting for their response. He was probably about thirty, tall, well-built and very good-looking, with a mop of dark curly hair, dark eyes, and a wide mobile mouth. Tessa's first coherent thought was that the new arrival looked like the ideal candidate for a holiday romance.

'Yes, of course. Please do,' gabbled Diane, on whom the newcomer had obviously had the same effect. He sat down gracefully and smiled at them.

'I'm Matt Dixon. Welcome to the hotel.'

43

They introduced themselves. Tessa was aware of the Spaniard they had snubbed glaring at them as he drained yet another gin.

'You're not the usual age-group,' was Matt's first comment, and this time they gave a fuller account of what had brought them to Spain in February. He sympathised and obviously thought that the holiday was a good idea.

'And what brought you here?' Tessa asked, eager to find out all about him.

'A tree fell on my house.' He laughed at their puzzled expressions. 'It's true. There was a gale one day and I came home to find that a large beech tree had blown down on my house, causing a lot of damage to the roof.'

'A beech tree? They can get very large. Have you got a big garden?' Tessa queried.

'Big enough for a bachelor,' he said casually. 'So then I had to find somewhere to stay while the house was repaired, and as I work with computers it meant that I could go anywhere

where there was a connection to the internet. So I came here.'

'You work with computers?'

'Programming, web-sites, that kind of thing,' he said vaguely.

The three of them sat together for the rest of the evening, talking, laughing, finding out what interests they had in common. The only disadvantage as far as Tessa was concerned was that Matt's gaze was usually fixed on Diane and her pale blonde hair. He was unfailingly polite, talking to both of them, listening when Tessa said something, but it was clear that it was Diane who really interested him.

'Oh, well,' thought Tessa, 'My first holiday romance will have to wait. I can always take photographs on the beach.'

The time passed pleasantly and unexpectedly rapidly, but the effect of the long day could not be ignored for ever. Soon after ten o'clock Tessa, after trying to stifle several yawns, announced that she was ready for bed. She would not have been surprised if Diane had decided to stay a little longer with Matt, but her friend admitted that she was also tired and they said good night to him, promising to meet again the next day, and left together. Most of the silver-haired hotel residents were still in the lounge, apparently ready to stay there till the bar closed at midnight. The young Spaniard was still slouched in his chair. Tessa had noticed that he had been drinking steadily throughout the evening and he almost snarled at the two girls as they passed him.

'You didn't have to come with me,' Tessa murmured to Diane. 'I thought you'd like the chance to spend a little time by yourself with Matt. He obviously fancies you.'

Diane smiled smugly.

'Yes, I got that impression too, but rule one in holiday romances is not to appear too keen at first. Anyway, I really am tired and I didn't want to fall asleep in front of him.'

'It's a pity he hasn't got a friend,'

Tessa could not resist adding wistfully.

'You never know. He seems a bright lad, so I wouldn't be surprised if he found someone somewhere to make up a foursome.' She gave a wicked grin. 'If not, there's always the Spaniard who tried to pick us up.'

'I'd rather stick to taking photographs!'

They both slept well and woke to find the sunlight streaming in the balcony window.

It must have taken some doing, but when they were inspecting the sunlit gardens and swimming-pool after a leisurely breakfast, Matt did indeed appear with another young man in tow. He was introduced as Gordon Welles. He was tall and thin, with a pale face, pale blue eyes, and fair hair. Privately, Tessa thought the best word to describe him was 'colourless', but decided not to make up her mind about him too quickly.

'I wasn't in the lounge last night as I went straight to bed after dinner,' he

47

explained to Tessa as Matt and Diane went off to fetch coffees for them all, Gordon insisting that his had to be decaffeinated.

'Oh, weren't you feeling well?' Tessa asked politely.

Apparently this was the reply he had hoped for, for he leant forward in his deck-chair, eager to tell her everything.

'It wasn't that I was ill yesterday,' he explained. 'It's just that I'm convalescent, recovering from a nasty attack of flu. That's why I'm here. I decided I really needed some warmth if I was to make a full recovery.' He sighed, rather dramatically. 'Unfortunately, I've always had a weak chest so I have to be careful to look after myself.'

Before he could go into any more detail, Matt and Diane returned with coffee and the conversation turned to other subjects, such as the sudden change in the weather.

'When we left the airport yesterday I thought we were doomed to a rain-soaked couple of weeks,' Diane said.

'But look at it now!' She waved an arm at the clear, brilliant blue sky and the calm sea.

'There has been the occasional rainy day, but mostly it's been sunshine,' Matt assured her.

'Which is just as well, because too much damp in the air gives me a chesty cough,' Gordon interjected.

After coffee, Matt suggested they should all go for a walk along the beach.

'Not for me,' Gordon said quickly. 'I don't want to risk getting my feet wet.'

'How about you girls?'

Matt spoke to both of them but he was looking at Diane, who looked uncertainly at Tessa, who in turn gave an unobtrusive nod of approval.

'I'd like that,' Diane said brightly.

'I'm a bit tired, so I'll stay here with Gordon,' Tessa said with noble self-sacrifice.

From his rather smug expression, this was obviously what Matt had intended and hoped for. As he had contrived to provide Tessa with Gordon for company he obviously felt he had fulfilled his obligation to her and was free to take Diane for a walk on her own. Once the other two had left, Gordon, happy to have a captive audience, gave Tessa a lot more unwanted information about his many health problems. Her heart sank as he went on and on. As well as his weak chest and his susceptibility to infections he also suffered from various allergies, so he had plenty to talk about. Tessa was very glad when Matt and Diane finally reappeared, looking very content in each other's company. The four of them had a light lunch at the hotel's beach-side café, where Gordon inspected the cutlery closely to make sure there were no lurking germs which might attack him. When they had finished Tessa insisted that according to Spanish custom she was going to have a siesta. It was at least a way of avoiding any more of Gordon's medical history for a while. Diane said cheerfully that it seemed a good idea and they went back to their room after arranging to meet the two young men for a drink before dinner.

'I'm afraid mine will be orange juice,' sighed Gordon. 'Alcohol affects my stomach.'

Tessa left quickly before he could go into more details and before she was driven to make some biting comment.

'I'm sorry about Gordon,' Diane said penitently in the privacy of their room. 'Apparently he's the only other young unattached male who is even remotely acceptable that Matt could find staying at the hotel, and even he's flying back to England tomorrow.'

Tessa cheered up at this news.

'I'm glad to hear it. Perhaps I can stand him for a few more hours.' She patted Diane's hand. 'I really don't mind if you and Matt want to go off by yourselves when Gordon's gone. I can explore the area. It's obviously got some very interesting places.'

Diane smiled at her gratefully.

'Of course I wouldn't desert you

completely,' she said warmly. 'But perhaps — once or twice — Matt and I would enjoy being just a twosome. We do seem to suit each other.'

'You really like him, don't you?'

Diane thought for a while, and then nodded.

'It's very early yet, of course, but he seems ideal for a holiday boyfriend. He's good-looking, amusing, intelligent, and he seems to think the same about me — which shows good judgement on his part.'

'But he's only good for a holiday romance?'

Diane shifted uneasily.

'I think so. He seems too good to be true, so I'm waiting for the drawbacks to appear. And I find his story about his house being wrecked but it doesn't matter because he can work anywhere so long as he has a computer just a little suspicious, so I'm going to be wary. I would have expected him to stay near the house to keep an eye on how the repair work is going, and he's rather vague about what he actually does with computers.' She thumped her pillow. 'Now, we are supposed to be having a sleep so we can look gorgeous later, so let's stop talking and have our siesta.'

It took an effort, but Tessa managed to endure the remaining hours with Gordon, mainly by firmly changing the subject most of the time when he started to talk about his health, and simply not listening when he did manage to launch forth on his physical weaknesses. She just hoped that Diane and Matt appreciated her self-sacrifice, and was glad when the time came to see him on the coach to the airport the next day. She waved goodbye to him as he left and gave a deep sigh of relief.

'Be careful on the plane,' she had warned him. 'Think of all the germs being given off in that confined space.'

'He probably thought me very unsympathetic,' she said as the coach drove off, prepared to feel guilty now she could do nothing about it.

'Don't worry,' commented Diane. 'I

expect he'll go home and tell all his friends that he met this girl called Tessa who thought he was marvellous and who was heartbroken when he left.' She looked round. 'Matt said he had some work to do but he promised me he'd be down soon.' She looked a little uncertain. 'Will you feel neglected, Tessa, if we go off by ourselves this afternoon? Matt and I do seem to be getting on so well, but I don't want to leave you on your own too much.'

'I'm fine,' Tessa assured her. 'I'm planning to walk along the beach and look for pretty pebbles when he does come.'

They found two sun beds in a shady corner, as their skin had not yet got accustomed to the strong Spanish sun. It was not yet warm enough for them to strip off too many clothes, but it was pleasant enough to sit outside. Diane could not relax, however, and was constantly fidgeting and looking towards the hotel door. In spite of the fact that she and Matt had met such a short time ago, she seemed to be growing very possessive.

The wait for Matt to appear was a lot longer than had been expected, and he was very apologetic when at last he came hurrying to find them.

'I thought it would be a quick job, but then I had an idea which took time to work out.'

Diane had been frowning impatiently but now she smiled forgivingly.

'So long as you weren't trying to avoid me.'

'I'd never do that,' he assured her, and Tessa began to wonder whether she would be able to find enough pretty pebbles and subjects for photography to keep herself occupied for the rest of the fortnight.

'The sun is so warm that I actually thought I might go for a swim,' Diane sighed, 'but when I put my hand in the pool it felt freezing still.'

'This is February,' Matt reminded her. 'Only the bravest go for a swim outdoors now.' He sat up, as if an idea had struck him. 'Of course, if you really feel like a swim we could go in the indoor pool. That's heated.'

Diane beamed.

'Yes, let's do that. It won't take me five minutes to change into my costume. Do you want to come, Tessa?'

Tessa shook her head.

'You two can go and be energetic. I'll just relax and think of Mr Briggs in that chilly little office in England.'

When the other two were out of sight she strolled down to the beach, to the water's edge, and gazed out to the horizon. She bent down and dipped her hand in the water. Somewhere over there this same sea was washing the shores of Africa, the Nile, and the Greek islands. Perhaps this trip to Spain was just the start and in the future she would explore other more exotic locations.

She decided to go back to her sun bed, where she lay back and closed her eyes, resolving she could go for a walk another time. All worries about the future temporarily forgotten, she felt herself gently drifting off to sleep. She was not left in peace for long, however.

'So the two of them have gone off and left you all alone? Don't worry. I am here to keep you company.'

Jerked back into alertness, Tessa sat up and looked round. The speaker was the young Spaniard whom she and Diane had snubbed after the first evening's dinner. Now he was sitting on one of the sun beds, smiling triumphantly at her. He had pulled his sun bed across so that she was trapped in a corner and could not get out without virtually clambering over him. As she could not escape him physically she decided to behave as if he were not there and lay down again, closing her eyes firmly. But he refused to be ignored. She felt his hand close over her wrist so hard that it almost hurt. She tried to pull herself free, but his grip tightened.

'Maybe we got off to a bad start, with your friend trying to make me look a fool, but that shouldn't stop us getting to know each other better — a lot better! I'm called Pedro Valdes, by the way. I'm here on my own and you might as well be, so let's make the best of it. I'm here because a branch of my father's business is here and he's sent me to give it some personal attention. That doesn't take up much of my time, but it does mean I've got a very generous expense account, so we can enjoy ourselves. What do you say?'

He grinned at her, obviously expecting her to be delighted by his attentions, but when she shook her head vigorously and tried to pull away his face darkened and his grip on her wrist became painful. He smiled as if he found pleasure in her obvious discomfort. She felt panicky, looking round for help, but nobody was near. She made a sudden effort and managed to wrench her arm free, taking him by surprise, and hastily moved as far away from him as she could.

'I am quite sure that I don't want

your company or your money, so will you please go away!' she hissed.

He glared at her.

'Don't be a fool!' Then, almost threateningly, 'I'm used to getting what I want.'

Tessa decided wildly that if the only way to escape was to throw a scene, to attack him physically if he would not let her pass, then that was what she would do, but before she could decide what to do next a new, cool, clear voice was heard.

'Do you need any help with this young man, my dear? He can be a nuisance.'

It was the woman who had spoken to Diane and Tessa in the lounge, assuring them that they could sit where they liked. Now she stood a couple of feet away, looking at the two of them enquiringly.

'Go away! We don't need your interference,' snapped the Spaniard.

'Yes, we do!' gasped Tessa. 'This — man — is pestering me. I want him to go away and leave me alone.'

'Then I'm sure he will. Otherwise, I shall have to go and tell the manager what is happening.'

'You wouldn't dare!' the young man declared, but there was an uncertain note in his voice and the woman looked at him coldly.

'Oh, but I will, and you know I am a woman of my word.'

He hesitated, glaring at her and then at Tessa, before he suddenly stood up and walked off. Tessa sighed with relief and almost collapsed on her sun bed.

'Thank you!' she said. 'Thank you very much indeed.'

'Not at all,' said the woman. 'I'm glad to help, especially if it upsets that unpleasant young man.'

She smiled and walked away before Tessa could say anything more.

Tessa could not relax after the incident and decided to go and rest in the privacy of her room and made for the lifts in the foyer. For some reason there was a delay before the lift arrived.

Tessa stood waiting impatiently. A man in workman's overalls and carrying a tool bag came to wait beside her. He looked at her, then smiled, and gave her a friendly nod, but Tessa had had enough of young men trying to accost her. She gave him a cold look and then ignored him pointedly. From the corner of her eye she saw him give a slight shrug. When the lift finally arrived he stood back and let her enter, but did not follow her. She was glad. It was bad enough having to be rescued from the attentions of Pedro Valdes. She certainly didn't want one of the hotel's workmen trying to pick her up.

Once in her room, she shut the door firmly, resisting the impulse to lock it, and flung herself on her bed. She found she was shaking and almost in tears, reacting to the unpleasant little scene with Valdes. She rubbed her wrist, bruised by his grasp, and found herself wishing that she was safely back in England under the shelter of her parents' roof.

When Diane came back she was extremely concerned to find Tessa huddled on the bed. Reassured that her friend was not feeling ill, she insisted on being told the cause of her depression, and was furious when she learnt how Pedro Valdes had behaved.

'Tell the manager!' she demanded. 'Get the horror thrown out of the hotel!'

Tessa, now sitting up, shook her head.

'I don't want to cause a public fuss. Anyway, I think he's learnt his lesson and will think twice before he tries to approach either of us.'

'I'll get Max to have a word with him,' Diane said grimly.

'No! That will only get Max into trouble.'

Diane put her arm round her friend.

'I almost feel that it's my fault. I persuaded you to come here, and then I left you alone while I went off with Max.'

'Please, Diane, let's forget about it.

I'm going to get up now, come downstairs and enjoy myself. I promise you that if Valdes comes near me I'll scream my head off.'

3

Tessa plodded grimly on along the dirt road between groves of trees. It was hot, small stones kept getting into her sandals, and she was pretty sure she was lost. The path she had taken had seemed at first to be going in the direction of the hotel, but then there had been a couple of unexpected twists and turns and now she didn't know where she was and was getting worried. Would she have to retrace her painful steps for the last mile or so? She brushed away some insect intent on attacking her face and her heart sank. She had come for a walk to explore the enormous orchards that covered so much of the area, partly from genuine curiosity, partly to leave Diane free to spend time with Matt without feeling guilty about neglecting her friend, and partly to be sure of avoiding any more unwelcome attention from the young Spaniard, Pedro Valdes. He had not tried to approach her since the incident by the swimming-pool, but at meal-times and in the lounge she had been conscious that he was often staring at her.

A small white van drove past her, and then slowed down. As she drew level with it she saw the driver waving to her, but she ignored him. No matter how tired and weary she felt, she had more sense than to accept a lift from a strange man! As it became clear that she was not going to stop, the van started up again and for a few yards drove slowly along beside her. She kept her face turned away and finally the driver seemed to accept her rejection and speeded up, disappearing round a bend in the road. She followed, reasoning that if the van was going somewhere, then possibly the path would link up with a proper road and she could find out where she was. But when she too had rounded the bend she saw that the road ended fifty yards ahead at a small, white-washed house. The van was parked in front of the house with the driver leaning against it. She was too exhausted to turn on her heels and hurry away so she drew nearer, cautiously, and stopped a few yards from him. Maybe, if he knew a little English, he could give her directions to the hotel.

He was about thirty, fair-haired and unshaven, dressed in jeans and a sweatshirt that had both seen better days. He was looking at her impatiently and said something in Spanish.

'What?' Tessa said. She shook her head. 'I don't speak Spanish,' she said very slowly and clearly.

He sighed impatiently.

'I was asking you what you wanted,' he said in English with just the hint of a Midlands accent. 'This is a private road leading to my house here, and when I saw you I assumed you were coming here to see me about something.'

Her shoulders sagged.

'I'm sorry. I'm lost, trying to get back to my hotel. I didn't mean to trespass.'

He shrugged.

'No problem. I just hoped you had work for me.'

He waved at the van. Tessa saw that it was painted with the words 'Tom Collins, Electrician and Plumber', together with some words in Spanish which she assumed was a translation, followed by a telephone number and an email address. She looked at the man again. He looked vaguely familiar and she suddenly realised that he was the workman she had seen by the lift the previous day. Fortunately he did not seem to have recognised her as the girl who had snubbed him.

'If you're trying to get to that big hotel on the beach you'll have to go back about a quarter of a mile and then take the turning to the left,' he informed her.

She closed her eyes in despair. Half a mile of wasted walking! The man must have seen her expression, for he took a step towards her, concern in his voice.

'Do you want to rest here for a while? You look as if you've had enough walking for a bit.'

She knew what a wreck she must look — dusty, dishevelled, sweaty and tired — but she did not want pity.

'Thank you, I can manage,' she said stiffly, and then turned, ready to make her painful way back along the road. She limped along for a few yards, then she twisted her foot on a loose stone and almost fell, but the man was beside her surprisingly quickly and held her upright, his arm around her waist. She stiffened at his touch and he released her and sighed resignedly.

'Hold on! I only came back to get some tools and have a cup of coffee. If you wait, I can give you a lift back to the hotel.'

She admitted to herself that It didn't matter if he was a stranger, she couldn't walk any further!

'Thank you,' she said again, this time with much more sincerity.

Tom Collins was looking at her carefully.

'You really do look tired out.'

She managed a smile.

'I didn't mean to walk so far, and sandals definitely weren't the best choice of footwear.'

He grinned sympathetically.

'Well, you may be an unexpected guest, but I can still be a polite host. Have a seat.' He pointed to a rough wooden table with two benches which stood nearby. 'Would you like a coffee or would you prefer a cold drink?'

Gratefully Tessa sank down on one of the benches.

'Coffee, please.'

'It will have to be black,' he warned her.

'That's fine. And no sugar.'

Tom Collins disappeared inside the house and she took off her sandals and shook out the loose gravel that had crept in, and then massaged her aching feet. He was soon back with a tray holding two mugs of coffee. He had also added a small plate of biscuits which he put on the table before taking his seat on the other bench. He watched as Tessa gratefully drank her coffee, her eyes closed as she savoured every refreshing drop.

'You're some way from the hotel,' he commented.

'I know I must be. I decided to explore the area, and it was fine for a while, but then I lost sight of the sea and all these trees look the same, whatever they are.'

He gestured at the trees around them.

'They're mostly avocadoes, but I've got some orange and lemon trees as well, mostly for my own use.'

'And some almonds,' she commented, gazing at the cloudy white flowers on a clump of trees. 'I can at least recognise those. So are you mainly an electrician or a farmer?'

'It depends on the day. If no one wants any electrical or plumbing work done then I'm a farmer. But I'm still doing up the house, so sometimes I'm a builder as well.'

'But you're English. How did you end up here?' She bit her lip. 'Sorry. I'm being nosy.'

'That's all right. It's a very short story. I learned my trade in England, but then I got bitten by the travel bug and wandered round Europe getting work where I could until I reached here. There was enough work to keep me occupied and after a few months I decided this was where I wanted to stay. My sister and her husband moved to Australia several years ago and my parents have gone to live there as well, so there was no reason for me to go back to England. I got the chance to buy this house and a few acres about two years ago. Both the house and the land were in a pretty bad state, so I got them fairly cheaply, but I've got a lot of work to do still.' He waved his arm at the house and the trees. 'For years I was really homeless, travelling from place to place, but now, when I come back here at the end of a day I know I am coming home, that this is where I belong.'

'But you are English. Don't you feel an outsider among the Spanish?'

He laughed and shook his head.

'No. I'm not like some of the English ex-pats who only socialise with other British people. I speak Spanish, I mix with the Spanish people, and I follow the Spanish way of life. As I said, I belong here.'

She had finished her coffee and reluctantly put the mug down on the table next to the untouched biscuits.

'Actually,' she said, looking down at her hands, 'now I've enjoyed your hospitality I have to admit that I owe you an apology.' He raised an eyebrow and she went on. 'We met at the hotel yesterday, by the lift, and I was a bit offhand, but that was because I'd just had an encounter with an unpleasant young Spaniard and was in a bad mood.'

He studied her face.

'Was it you? I thought I'd seen you

before, though I wasn't sure. Don't worry about it, I didn't. Incidentally, was the unpleasant young man called Valdes?'

'Yes! Have you met him?'

He grimaced.

'I know the hotel manager, and I do work for him when the usual plumber is not available, and I was there about a week ago when I had to rescue one woman from Valdes' over-eager attentions.' He smiled suddenly. 'I threatened to punch him if he didn't stop pestering her and he almost ran away. I think he was definitely under the influence of something — drink or even drugs. He is a nasty piece of work, and I'm not surprised you were upset.'

There seemed nothing else to talk about after that, and Tessa tried to stand up. She winced as she took her weight on her sore, bare feet.

'Well, thank you for your hospitality. You don't have to take me to the hotel if it's inconvenient.'

'I think you've definitely done enough

walking for one day so I will give you a lift back. It'll only take five minutes.'

She was relieved, really too exhausted to raise any more polite objections, but at that moment there was a sudden burst of electronic music. Tom Collins took out his mobile.

'Tom Collins.'

He listened for a minute or so, nodding occasionally, said something in Spanish, and ended the call. He looked at Tessa wryly.

'I'm afraid that's an urgent call for help from a lady who has water flooding her kitchen, and she wants me there as soon as possible.'

'Then thank you again for your hospitality and the offer of a lift, and I'll walk back.'

But when she tried to put her sandals on again her feet refused to fit in them. She tried again, conscious of Tom Collins watching her, but it was no use.

'I think my feet have swollen,' she was forced to admit. 'But don't mind me. I'll just sit here for a while, if you don't mind, until they feel better.'

'Or you could come with me to see Senora Ceballos. From what she said, it won't be a long job, and I could drive you back to the hotel afterwards.'

She wanted to get back to the hotel and relax in comfort, not be driven around in an old van and then have to wait while some woman's plumbing problems were solved, but she looked at her feet, then at the rough path. There didn't seem to be any choice.

'If you don't mind too much, I'll come with you.'

She was glad to climb into the little van though the springs in the seat had almost worn through the fabric and there was a screech as Tom Collins put it into gear. He looked apologetic.

'This was all I could afford when I started up my business, and I'm a better plumber than I am a mechanic.'

He drove them along narrow roads for about ten minutes to the front door of a house surrounded by carefully-tended gardens where he helped her to clamber out a little stiffly, just as the front door was flung open and a comfortably-built lady of about forty appeared, welcoming them with a flood of Spanish that clearly showed her relief that help had arrived. Tom responded in the same language. Finally he switched back to English.

'I have explained to the senora why you are here and I've asked her to look after you while I fix the leak.'

Then he reached into the van, hauled out a bag of tools, and vanished into the house, leaving Tessa to wonder how she was going to communicate with her hostess, who had decided she need not worry about the flooded kitchen now Tom Collins was here and had instead turned her attention to Tessa and was now obviously welcoming her.

'I'm sorry, I don't know Spanish,' Tessa confessed, and to her relief Senora Ceballos addressed her in English, accented but understandable.

'Please, come and sit down in the garden.'

At the back of the house she pointed to a white-painted wrought iron table with two chairs, indicated that Tessa should take one chair and left her to gaze at the magnificent view over a wooded valley while her hostess disappeared inside the house but soon reappeared with a tray bearing a jug of fresh orange juice and two glasses.

When the juice had been sipped and approved, Senora Ceballos turned to Tessa, obviously curious about her.

'You are a friend of Tom's?' she enquired.

Tessa shook her head.

'I only met him today. He saw I had walked too far, and he is going to take me back to my hotel when he has mended your leak.' There was a short silence. 'Have you known him long?' was all Tessa could think of saying.

'Since they came here, over two years ago. I was one of his first customers.'

'They?'

Senora Ceballos face grew sad and she shook her head mournfully.

'Tom and Lucia — they came together — but then Lucia died. When I saw you, I hoped that perhaps Tom had found someone else at last. Now, I must leave you for a little while.'

Tessa sat enjoying the orange juice and the view, wondering about Tom Collins and the girl friend he had lost, until Tom came out of the house, wiping his hands on a rag. Senora Ceballos reappeared and Tom took her back into the house to inspect his work. They soon returned, Senora Ceballos obviously full of gratitude.

'The senora can mop up her floor now and I can take you back to your hotel,' Tom told Tessa.

There were a couple of minutes of hand-shaking and kisses, and then Tessa was back in the van, finally being driven towards the hotel.

'That didn't take long,' Tessa commented.

'No. Fortunately it just needed a joint

tightened and I put some tape round it to make sure.'

She stole a look at him. He looked practical and down-to-earth, not like a man who had somehow lost the woman he loved.

The hotel soon appeared and Tom drew up at the front door and once again helped Tessa out of the van.

'Thank you for the lift and your hospitality, and I hope you soon finish your house,' she told him. 'If it wasn't for you, I'd still be hopelessly lost and in too much pain to walk.'

'Glad to be of help.'

He smiled, waved farewell, then drove away without looking back. She turned and stopped abruptly as she saw Pedro Valdes standing at the top of the steps which led to the hotel entrance, watching her. He had obviously seen her arrival with Tom Collins, but she lifted her chin and walked past him without acknowledging his presence and he made no attempt to accost her. She went into the hotel in search of

Matt and Diane and found them lying on sun-beds in the garden, but Diane sat up when she saw Tessa.

'So there you are at last! You've been gone ages.' She took off her sunglasses so she could examine her friend more closely and her voice rose. 'What's happened to you? You're limping and you look exhausted.'

Tessa sank down beside them and told them of her day's adventure.

'So I was rescued by a man in a white van instead of a knight on a white horse,' she finished.

'You were taking a risk,' Diane scolded her. 'You should have turned round and walked away when you saw him waiting for you.'

'Stop sounding like my mother. What good would that have been? There was just him and me and hundreds of avocado trees. No, Mr Collins is more interested in his house and possible work than in lost young ladies.'

Anyway, she admitted to herself as she looked in the mirror a little later before stripping and heading for the shower, her rescuer was unlikely to have found her dusty, limp appearance at all attractive.

The next morning she, Matt and Diane were just about to start on a walk to the small town about a mile from the hotel when to her surprise she recognised the little white van as it drew up in the hotel drive. As Tom Collins climbed out she waved at him. He stared at her blankly, obviously not immediately recognising the fresh, neatly-dressed girl as the tired wreck of the day before. Then recognition dawned, and he walked towards them. She saw that today he was wearing clean jeans and a fresh white and blue striped shirt, and that he had shaved, and she felt guiltily relieved that her friends were seeing a much more presentable version than the sweat-stained workman of the previous day. Matt and Diane regarded him with surprised interest as he approached them. He stopped a few feet away, smiling at Tessa and then glancing at her friends. Tessa turned to them.

'Diane — Matt — let me introduce you to Tom Collins, the man who rescued me when I was hopelessly lost yesterday.'

'So you're Tessa's saviour. She was very grateful to you,' Diane commented.

'It was the least I could do,' Tom said politely.

'Have you come to see how she survived?' Matt enquired.

Tom shook his head.

'I do work for the hotel occasionally and I've nothing on today so I decided to come to have a word with the manager before I go back to the farm.' He looked at their clothes, obviously more suited to the town than the beach. 'Are you going somewhere?'

'We're going for a walk around town,' Diane told him.

'You'll enjoy that,' Tom assured her. 'It is a very pleasant place, not too noisy or touristy.'

An idea had been forming in Tessa's mind, a way of escaping from the trip with Diane and Matt.

'I did enjoy what I saw of your farm yesterday,' she said brightly. 'I'd like to see more of it some time — when you're free.'

Tom Collins blinked, and then looked from Tessa to Matt and Diane, who were holding hands, and finally he responded as she had hoped. Indeed, she supposed she'd left him little choice.

'As I said, I haven't got anything on for the rest of the day after I've called here, so I'll soon be going home. Would you like to come back with me now? You could have lunch at my house and then I could show you what I've done to the buildings and land so far.'

Tessa didn't really find the prospect of a few hours discussing house repairs at all exciting, and was not interested in Mr Collins as a possible companion for the holiday, but he was a reasonably presentable young man who was willing to spend a couple of hours with her. That was good for her ego. More importantly, it also meant that she wouldn't have to trail round town with Diane and Matt, because no matter how good their intentions, there were times when they would stand close together, bodies almost touching, murmuring to each other, completely forgetting her, and at such times she wished she was miles away. Listening to a lecture on damp-courses and bricklaying might just be preferable, if she had to.

'Thank you, I'd like that,' she told him. 'And it should be easier on my poor feet than walking round town.'

His smile grew wider.

'I warn you, I can get quite eloquent on the techniques of plastering.'

'I'll risk it,' she laughed.

Matt and Diane set off together while Tessa waited by the van for Tom to go and see the manager. He was back in five minutes, and as he was helping her into the van there was the noise of a powerful engine starting up close by, and an open-topped sports car swept past them, nearly brushing Tom aside. It roared out on to the main road without stopping to look for oncoming traffic. Tessa had a glimpse of Pedro Valdes driving it. Well, he wouldn't be able to annoy her that morning.

'Perhaps he's actually going to do some work for his father,' she said hopefully.

'I can't imagine him helping any business.'

It only took the van a few minutes to cover a stretch of the main road, turn off, and start negotiating the dirt tracks.

'What happens to these roads when it rains?' she asked.

'They turn into miniature rivers. Once I was trapped in the house for three days because the roads were impassable. Fortunately the land drains well, so it doesn't happen very often.'

City-bred Tessa shuddered at the idea of such a primitive situation, but she forgot the drawbacks of rural life when she saw the little white house again. It was bathed in sunshine and looked very snug.

Once out of the van, she turned to face Tom, having decided that honesty was the best policy.

'Look, I'm sorry, but when I said I wanted to look round your house I didn't really mean it.'

He raised his eyebrows in mock surprise, then smiled wickedly.

'I understand. It wasn't the house, it was the owner that attracted you.'

His smile became a leer and he took a step towards her. She retreated, hands held out in front of her in self-defence, suddenly feeling that she had made a very big mistake.

'Well, I don't mind that at all . . . ,' he murmured.

'No!' she exclaimed. 'You don't understand!'

But now he was suddenly shaking with real laughter. She looked at him in bewilderment.

'I understand perfectly,' he told her.

'You didn't want to go round town playing gooseberry to that pair, so you used me as an excuse to get away from them. It was pretty clear, you know.'

She looked a little shame-faced.

'Yes, and I'm sorry. You don't have to bother about me. I'll walk back to the hotel now.'

'What happens when they ask you questions about the house?'

'I'll think of something to tell them.'

He was shaking his head.

'No. You owe me a few minutes of your time. I like my house and I like telling people about it, and I'm not going to let a captive audience escape.' He shrugged. 'Come on. It will be better than wandering around by yourself, and you might actually enjoy it — and you'll get lunch.'

Tessa looked at the farmhouse again. He was right. The least she could do was listen to him — or appear to listen.

'It does look like something out of a fairy tale,' she told the proud owner. 'Please, do show me round.'

87

The tour of the house did not take long, and to her surprise she found it interesting. There was a biggish room on the ground floor which served as living room and kitchen, with a sink and a small Calor gas stove in one corner. Tom pointed out a wood-burning stove that provided heat in cold weather, when the oven it incorporated could be used for baking.

'Not that I do much cooking. I can survive on cold meat, cheese, bread and fruit. A friend of mine has a restaurant not far away, so if I feel like eating something different I go there.'

Oil lamps apparently provided lighting in the evening when required.

'Is that enough?' Tessa enquired, looking doubtfully at the ancient lamps.

'I'm usually up very early in the morning and in bed soon after sunset, so I don't need much light.'

A small outbuilding attached to the back of the house provided basic bathroom facilities. Tom Collins saw her carefully neutral expression and grew defensive.

'As you can see, I've got solar panels and they give me hot water. The water itself comes from a spring of pure water I've piped. Now, let me show you the bedrooms.'

She followed him slowly, reflecting that her mother would have been screaming warnings at this point, but his face was shining with the pride of ownership, not passion.

Upstairs there were two bedrooms, one of them almost filled with an enormous double bed.

'How on earth did you get that up here?' Tessa marvelled.

Tom grinned.

'Fortunately I didn't have to. The iron bedstead had been left here — probably because it would have taken too much work to dismantle it to get it out of the house — so all I had to do was get rid of the rust, repaint it, and find a mattress and some sheets.'

She did not comment on the

photograph of a dark-haired, smiling girl which stood on a table near the bed.

The whole house, inside and out, was whitewashed and very clean.

They returned to the sunlit table and benches outside.

'And you live here by yourself?' she enquired, wondering whether anyone had tried to replace Lucia.

'It's still pretty primitive. I can't see anybody else wanting to share it with me.'

It struck her that he might actually harbour a faint hope that she was there because she did find him attractive and might even be considering what it would be like to live there herself, so she hastened to disillusion him.

'I can understand that. I wouldn't like to live in such an isolated spot without even electricity. I like my comforts.'

His look was definitely cold.

'Some day I expect I'll meet a girl who appreciates the countryside and will know how to help me.'

Now they had each made it crystal clear where they stood.

The tour now over, Tom remembered his duties as host.

'I promised you lunch, but don't expect a feast. I've already told you that I don't do much cooking.'

He disappeared back into the house to emerge in a few minutes carrying the improvised meal, which consisted of the cold meats, cheese and bread that he had talked about.

'It looks good,' Tessa said appreciatively, beginning to realise how long it had been since breakfast.

'Wait a minute. There's something else.'

He hurried round a corner of the house and reappeared holding aloft a dripping bottle of white wine.

'It's been cooling in the stream. Now it's just the right temperature.'

It made a very pleasant picnic. For dessert he produced an old biscuit tin which he opened triumphantly to reveal some small fruit tarts.

'From Manuel's restaurant,' he informed her. They were delicious.

During the meal conversation was still about the house.

'You see that outbuilding attached to the end of the house? That used to be a stable, but I'm planning to convert it into another bedroom and a proper bathroom. I might be able to rent it out to holiday-makers in the summer.'

'How long is all this going to take you?'

'It depends how much work I get elsewhere, and that will decide when I can afford to do things. But I don't have to worry about time. I can please myself.' He remembered something else. 'I hope to be able to generate electricity within the year. Then I can get a refrigerator and a washing machine.'

'And a television and a telephone?'

'Possibly. At the moment I'm usually too tired by evening to want to watch television, and I manage with a mobile phone and a laptop computer with a gadget that lets me connect to the internet. Coverage is very good round here.'

She asked about his travels before he had settled on the farm, and listened fascinated to stories about the many places he had visited.

'But finally I came here, mainly because I was with someone who had spent her holidays here as a child, and who loved it.'

'Senora Ceballos told me about Lucia,' Tessa said quietly. 'I'm sorry.'

He was silent for a minute, then sighed.

'It was some virus. Lucia wasn't feeling well, but it didn't seem anything to worry about. To tell the truth, I thought she might be pregnant, and I'd already started day-dreaming about raising children here. Then one day she collapsed and had to be rushed to hospital, and she died a few hours later.'

'And have you chosen to stay here

because it's a link with her?'

'At first, maybe, but now I live here because I love the area.' He stirred. 'We were together for nearly three years, and we were very happy. Then after Lucia died, I thought at first, of course, that I'd never get over it. I thought about her every day — every hour — but then the pain finally started to ease. I'll never forget her, that would be impossible, but as time passes I have found myself making plans for the future instead of just brooding on the past.'

There was another silence before Tessa decided it was time to change the subject.

'Do you feel safe here by yourself?' she enquired.

'Perfectly safe. After all, I haven't got anything that anyone would want to steal.' He hesitated. 'It's funny you should say that, however. You remember I put out some biscuits yesterday but we didn't eat them? Well, when I got back here after taking you to the hotel the biscuits had all gone.'

'The birds must have taken them.'

'Possibly. But there were no crumbs or broken bits, so they must have been very tidy birds. And yesterday I found some orange peel under the trees, and birds certainly don't peel fruit.'

Lunch was finished, and for a time they were content to just sit in the sunshine in a companionable silence, till Tom stirred and looked at his watch.

'Would you like to complete the tour and look round my fruit trees?'

He cleared the food and dirty dishes off the table but just put the lid back on the remaining two fruit tarts.

'That should keep any greedy birds out, and we can eat them when we get back.'

4

During the tour of his property Tom pointed out the different fruit trees, including some she had scarcely heard of, such as custard apples, and she was almost disappointed when they finished and returned to the house.

'You've listened very patiently,' Tom said appreciatively, 'and as a reward I'll make us a cup of tea now, proper English tea. That's one thing I can't give up.'

Tessa expected the tea to be served in the mugs used for yesterday's coffee, but he brought out a tray with proper cups and saucers, a milk jug and sugar basin.

'I begged some fresh milk from the hotel manager yesterday evening,' he told her as he poured out the tea and then picked up the biscuit tin. 'We might as well finish off the fruit tarts.'

He took the lid off, peered in, frowned, and then wordlessly held the tin out for her to see. It was empty. He sat back, and they looked at each other in bewilderment.

'A bird can't take a lid off a tin and then put it back,' he said grimly.

Tessa gazed around, suddenly feeling cold, wondering if unseen eyes were watching them.

'What do you think has happened? What can you do?'

His lips tightened, and his voice was unexpectedly loud when he spoke.

'Time for me to take you back to the hotel now, Tessa.'

Quickly, unceremoniously, leaving the tea things on the table, he strode over to his van and Tessa followed him. Tom must have decided it would be best to take her back to the security of the hotel before he investigated the mystery. She was shocked by the abrupt end to her visit, wondering what or who was taking the food, and rather glad to be getting away from a spot where such strange things were happening. But a few hundred yards away, around the bend that hid his house, Tom stopped the van and switched off the engine. She looked at him in surprise.

'I'm going back to the house and I can cut back through the trees from here,' he said in a low voice. 'If anybody is lurking near the house I may be able to catch them unawares. Do you want to come with me or would you rather stay here?'

She scrambled out of the van.

'I'm coming with you! I want to solve the mystery of the disappearing tarts.' And, she added mentally, she didn't want to be left by herself.

Taking care to avoid stepping on twigs or brushing against the lower branches, Tom led her as quickly and quietly as possible through the trees and back towards the house. As they cautiously approached it, still hidden by the dense foliage, Tom took her by the wrist and gestured to her to stand beside him. Together they peered out across the open space. Tessa gasped as she saw a small figure kneeling on one of the benches, drinking the remaining milk straight from the jug and too absorbed in what it was doing to realise it had been discovered till it was too late to escape. Tom rushed across the space, silently light-footed, and clamped his arms round its waist. There was a shrill scream and Tom found himself clutching a kicking, biting and scratching bundle of fury, but he tightened his hold so that his victim had less room to struggle. Now he and Tessa were able to see his captive properly and realise that he was holding a little girl about six years old. But before either of them could say anything, another small figure hurtled round the corner of the house, shouting incoherently, and launched itself at Tom, almost knocking him over with the force of its impetus. Now it was Tessa's turn to go into action and she seized the little girl from Tom, leaving him free to deal with the new assailant. The fight was hopelessly one-sided and soon Tom was holding a young boy by the scruff of the neck at arm's length so that the kicks and punches being directed at him had little impact. Seeing the rescue attempt had failed, the little girl stopped struggling and collapsed, sobbing, in Tessa's arms.

'Make sure she doesn't get away,' Tom instructed curtly as he pulled the boy over to the bench, sat him down firmly and stood in front of him, hands on hips. The little girl suddenly broke free from Tessa's grasp and ran towards the boy, scrambling on to the bench beside him. The two dark-haired children, both dressed in old jeans and T-shirts and so alike that they were obviously brother and sister, looked at Tom apprehensively, the boy putting his arm protectively round the girl's shoulders.

'So — two little thieves,' Tom said ominously.

Then he switched to Spanish, but the

boy shook his head, refusing to answer, until the little girl said something to Tom which obviously took him aback.

'What did she say?' Tessa asked.

'She said she was hungry.'

Now suddenly the boy was pouring out a torrent of words and Tom turned to Tessa.

'He says they haven't eaten much in two days. He's sorry they took the biscuits and tarts but they were very hungry and we didn't seem to want them.'

They looked at the two children. All signs of defiance had vanished. The boy's shoulders were sagging, his lip was trembling as though he was about to burst into tears, and the children were holding on to each other desperately for comfort and mutual support. Tom sighed.

'Whatever they've done, it appears we've got two hungry children on our hands. Let's feed them.'

While Tessa watched the children to make sure they did not try to run away,

Tom went into the house and rustled up some soup and bread, as well as the meat and cheese left over from their lunch. He put it on the table and the children looked at it with longing. He crooked a finger at them and then pointed to the food. They needed no more encouragement but attacked it ravenously and did not stop eating till every scrap had gone, carefully picking up the crumbs and licking them off their fingers.

'Now perhaps we can get a bit more information out of them,' said Tom grimly.

It took a little while. Tom questioned the boy, receiving brief answers in reply at first, but then the child launched on a long speech and Tom listened, only occasionally interrupting to clarify a point. At last he was ready to tell Tessa.

'The boy is called Juan. He's nine years old, and his sister Maria is six. Their mother is dead and their father couldn't find enough work where they lived, some distance north of here, so recently he brought them south hoping to get work in the tourist areas on the coast. Apparently they've been living for about a week in a tent in some rough ground just outside my property. Then, two days ago, their father went out to look for work and just didn't come back. They didn't dare go looking for him because he'd made them promise to stay near their tent, and in any case they were afraid that he might come back when they were gone.' He looked at the children with pity. 'Apparently he hadn't left them with much food and they've been surviving on what little they had and fruit from the trees. Then they found the biscuits outside this house yesterday and came back today hoping to find more and they were delighted to find the two tarts.'

Tessa looked at the children with an aching heart.

'What do you think could have happened to their father?'

An elaborate shrug.

'It could be any one of a number of

things. He could have had an accident, or drowned his sorrows at a bar and ended up in a police cell.' He hesitated. 'Or he could have got tired of looking after two small children and just abandoned them.'

Tessa stared at him with horror.

'He couldn't have just left them in the woods to starve!'

'We don't know how desperate he was.'

'Look at their clothes. They're well-worn but they're not shabby or neglected. I don't believe they were abandoned deliberately.'

'The question is, what to do with them now? Well, obviously I can't leave them to fend for themselves in the woods, so I think that first of all I'm going to take them to their tent. I'll collect whatever is in it and bring it back here.' He looked at her apologetically. 'I invited you out for lunch and a look round the place. I didn't mean to get you involved in all this. If you like, I'll put us all in the van and take you back to the hotel before I go tent-hunting.'

'Nonsense! You can't deal with the two of them on your own. I'm coming with you.'

His gratitude was wordless but clear.

Guided by the children, they soon found the tent, a small, basic affair which could barely have held its three occupants at night. Inside were two holdalls containing mostly clothes, though they found a few documents in a side pocket. Leaving the tent where it was for the time being, Tessa and Tom carried a holdall each back to his house, the children chatting happily beside them. Now he had fed them, Juan and Maria seemed to have decided that in the absence of their father Tom was a good substitute. Back at his home, Tom and Tessa took the documents out and spread them on the table to see what they could learn.

'These may be private papers,' Tom commented, 'but we need more information if we are to help these two.'

There was an envelope containing a few photographs. Some of them were obviously pictures of the children when they were smaller and one photograph showed a young couple. The woman was tenderly holding a baby, while a little boy held his father's hand. Juan saw them looking at it and joyfully started pointing at the figures, clearly identifying them.

'It's the family before their mother died,' translated Tom. 'At least we now have some idea of what his father looks like.'

Tessa looked at the proud, happy face of the man in the photograph and wondered how much the loss of his wife and his recent experiences would have changed him.

'I suppose I'll have to inform the authorities about them, and they will decide what to do with them,' said Tom. He looked at his watch and sighed in disgust. 'All the offices will be closed now. Well, they'll just have to stay here for the night. I haven't got any work lined up for tomorrow morning so I'll be able to contact the authorities as soon as they open. Do you think they'll trust me enough to stay with me tonight?'

But when he told the children that he proposed they should spend the night with him they received the news that they were to be his guests with big smiles of delight, and raced upstairs to inspect the bedrooms. In no time they were bouncing up and down on the great double bed. It would obviously be a big improvement on sleeping on the ground in the tiny tent.

'No, that's my bed!' Tom protested, but they took no notice. 'Oh, well, there's a camp bed in the other room,' he said resignedly.

Now Tessa looked at her watch.

'It will be dinner at the hotel soon,' she said worriedly. 'Do you think you could give me that lift back that you offered earlier?'

'Of course!' Tom said warmly, and then hesitated. 'About these two

— tomorrow — I don't know if you . . . '

'I'll be here tomorrow morning early,' she interrupted him. 'Of course I want to know what happens. This is far more interesting than sitting on a beach by myself.'

He smiled at her warmly.

'I'll be grateful for your help.'

His smile was one of his best points, Tessa decided after he had left her at the hotel door and driven away with the children waving out of the back window. Maybe he wasn't as immediately attractive as Matt, but he was well-built and his face benefited from a good chin and a neat nose. He was also kind and caring. The children would be safe with him.

She turned back to the hotel, reminding herself that this was where she was supposed to be spending her holiday.

Diane was in their room, carefully applying mascara, when Tessa walked in. She raised an eyebrow and smiled.

'It must have been a good lunch. Was the house so interesting?'

'The situation became complicated,' Tessa sighed, sinking into a chair. She suddenly realised how tiring the day had been. 'I've been hunting tart-snatchers and feeding abandoned children.'

Diane dropped the mascara and demanded details and Tessa told her the story of the day.

'Definitely not what you were expecting,' commented Diane. 'No wonder you look exhausted. A shower before dinner will make you feel better and you really look as if you need it. Mr Tom Collins doesn't return you in good condition, does he? We can go into dinner late.'

'What about Matt? Won't he be waiting for you?'

A shadow crossed her friend's face.

'Matt's working — again. After we got back from town and had lunch I was looking forward to an afternoon by the pool with him, but then he announced that he had to catch up with something he's doing for an English firm and vanished! I spent the afternoon with two old dears who insisted on telling me their life histories.'

'Well, Matt's not really here on holiday like us, is he? He's using the hotel as his place of work as well as somewhere to stay while his house is repaired.' She decided to change the subject. 'Did you enjoy looking round the town?'

Diane's face lit up.

'It was charming! There are lots of little winding streets with lovely shops and Matt bought me a present. Look!'

She thrust out her right hand. A ring glittered on a finger of her right hand. Tessa was taken aback.

'I thought this was just a holiday romance, Diane. If he's buying you expensive jewellery . . . '

Diane was laughing.

'Don't be silly! It's just a bit of costume jewellery, a bit of bling, though we did buy it in a proper jeweller's

110

shop. Here!' She slipped the ring off and handed it to Tessa. 'You try it on.'

Tessa did as she said, twisting her hand so that the blue stone caught the light. Then she took it off and examined it closely.

'There are some marks on it, Diane. Are you sure they're not hallmarks?'

Diane shook her head firmly.

'Matt and I have definitely clicked, but we haven't reached the stage where he would buy me expensive presents, and I wouldn't take them if he did.'

Tessa gave the ring back, still not quite convinced, and then disappeared to have her shower. Matt was not to be seen when they started dinner, and Diane complained at some length that there was little point in having a holiday romance with a man who kept disappearing for hours on end. Fortunately, before Tessa could tell her how boring she was getting, Matt appeared just as they were finishing their main course.

'I decided the client could wait an extra couple of hours because I wanted to be with you,' he explained to Diane, who lost her sulky look and glowed with pleasure.

After coffee in the lounge, Matt, his eyes on Diane, suggested going down to the beach to see the effect of the moonlight on the sea.

'Why don't you two go?' Tessa suggested, as she knew she was expected to. 'I've had a tiring day.'

Matt and Diane didn't try to persuade her and quickly disappeared. Tessa snuggled down in her comfortable chair. She was sleepy and the next day would probably be exhausting so she would enjoy an early night. She wondered how Tom was coping with the two children and what would happen to them the next day. Perhaps it had been a mistake to offer to help the following morning. After all, it was nothing to do with her. She wondered if Tom would be able to cope if she simply didn't appear.

'May I join you? We both seem to be on our own tonight.'

It was the woman who had spoken to them on the first evening and who had helped repel the young Spaniard. Tessa welcomed her with a smile.

'Please sit down. My friends have gone to admire the moonlight,' she said, and the woman laughed.

'It sounds very romantic, and the two of them do seem to be getting on well together from what I've seen. My friends are playing bridge again, and I'm afraid I soon get bored with that. My name's Rose Hunt, by the way.'

Once Rose Hunt had settled in her chair, Tessa said quietly, 'I haven't had an opportunity to thank you properly for helping to get rid of that horrible Pedro Valdes.'

'I was glad to be able to help upset that detestable young man. He even made advances to me some days ago. Apparently he thought that at my age I'd be grateful for any attention from a younger man.'

'What happened?'

'Well, he'd got me trapped in a quiet

113

corner of the lounge, a bit like he trapped you. I said that if he didn't let me pass, I'd scream. He didn't believe I meant it.'

'So?'

'I screamed,' Rose Hunt said with great satisfaction. 'Dozens of people came rushing over to see what was the matter and Mr Valdes vanished with the speed of light. I told everyone that I thought I'd seen a rat, but that I must have been mistaken, or it had run away. Plenty of people grasped what I was really referring to and he hasn't troubled me since.'

Rose Hunt was intelligent and amusing, and Tessa enjoyed her conversation. She explained why she and Diane were holidaying in Spain in February, and her companion was very sympathetic.

'I know how your life can be suddenly disrupted.' Her voice was suddenly sad. 'Two years ago I was playing golf with my husband. He hit the ball and stood watching it soar away. 'A good shot,' he said, and then he just fell to the ground. It was a heart attack and it killed him instantly.' Her face was set and she was staring into the distance as if visualising the scene. 'I'll always regret that I didn't get a chance to say goodbye to him. Then I had to deal with the aftermath. Unfortunately I didn't just lose my husband. He was in his early fifties, doing very well, but we hadn't really got round to planning our finances for when he retired, and our nice income died with him. I sold our house and bought a small flat, so I can manage, but there isn't much to spare. Some friends have been very supportive, but others find it difficult to fit a woman on her own into their social life, and I can't really entertain properly in my flat. So my big treat is a month off-season here where it's warm and I don't have to cook or clean.' She gave a twisted smile. 'I'm sorry. I didn't mean to tell you my sad story.'

'Not at all. You seem to have coped

very well. Do you always come here by yourself?'

'Yes. It's quite easy to get friendly with the other older guests, and I can always go to my room and read if I get too bored.'

Soon afterwards Diane reappeared, on her own, and was introduced to Rose Hunt. She was polite, but seemed a little disgruntled because Matt had left her again. Tessa decided to remind her of Matt's good points.

'Show Rose your ring, Diane.' She turned to Rose. 'It's a present from Matt. Isn't it pretty?'

Rose Hunt looked at the ring as Diane held her hand out, then leant forward and examined it more closely.

'It's a very nice ring indeed.'

'Just a souvenir,' Diane said dismissively.

Rose Hunt looked at Tessa as if she would like to say more, but as Diane continued to sit sulkily quiet she soon excused herself and went off to her room.

'You weren't very friendly, Diane,' Tessa said reprovingly.

'I'm sorry. I'll be nicer the next time I see her.'

'So what's upset you? Where's Matt?'

'Matt has gone back to his computing. He says he's going to work through the night and seemed to think I should be very grateful because he spared me a couple of hours!'

'Oh dear! Maybe it's just as well that he's only a holiday romance.'

'He won't even be that for the rest of the holiday if he's not careful.'

Matt did not appear for breakfast, and when Tessa reminded Diane that she was going back to the farm to help Tom Collins with the children, her friend did not take it well.

'I don't see why you should leave me on my own just to help some stranger with a couple of stray kids,' she grumbled.

Tessa felt a momentary touch of guilt at leaving Diane alone until she remembered how Diane had not hesitated to abandon her in order to be with Matt.

'I told him I'd go,' she said quietly, and Diane sniffed disdainfully.

'I think he's got a cheek asking you to go back. After all, he knows you're supposed to be enjoying a comfortable holiday here. He probably doesn't think you'll turn up.'

'Nevertheless, I'm going.'

Diane looked at her sharply.

'You don't really care about the children, do you? It's Tom Collins. It gives you an excuse to see him again.'

'I don't care about Tom Collins! I wouldn't care if I never saw him again, but I do want to know what happens to the children.'

But her friend was nodding, satisfied that she had guessed right.

'Oh, well, in that case I suppose I'll just have to sit here by myself. I'll be all right.'

Her martyred expression did not quite go with her words.

'After all, you weren't to know that

I'd be left by myself while Matt plays with his computer. I could go shopping in town . . . ' Diane hesitated. 'I suppose there is the possibility that Matt may emerge some time. I'd better stay here.'

Suddenly she hugged Tessa impulsively.

'I'm sorry I'm being such a misery. It's just that I do like Matt a lot and we'll only have this fortnight together. Go off and enjoy yourself.'

Tessa hugged her back.

'I don't think you'd mind about Matt's absences so much if you didn't care about him,' she observed.

Diane nodded slowly.

'I hate to admit it, but I think you may be right. When we are together — when he touches me — I feel I never want to be apart from him.' She shrugged impatiently. 'But in a few days we'll say goodbye, so I just wish he would stop vanishing. It's wasting precious time!'

It took Tessa about half an hour to

walk to the farm now she knew the way. She had dressed in jeans, T-shirt and sensible shoes, but the skies were threatening rain, and she was glad to arrive without getting wet. Tom managed a smile in greeting, but he looked preoccupied. The two children did not greet Tessa. They were sitting huddled together and there were signs of recent tears on Maria's cheeks. Clearly things were not going smoothly.

'Am I glad to see you! I'm not used to getting two children washed and dressed, and then after breakfast I told them that I would have to take them to the authorities and say that they needed looking after because their father has disappeared,' Tom murmured discreetly. 'They were very upset. Maria was in floods of tears and Juan said they wanted to stay here with me till their father came back. But I can't get them to understand that I can't look after them any longer! I'd probably be accused of kidnapping them. They're not my responsibility and I know nothing about looking after children. Anyway, I've got to go to work most days. The sooner I can hand them over to someone else, the better.'

'Who will you go to?'

'If I go to the police station first, they should be able to tell me the right people to contact.'

He turned and spoke to the children. Juan nodded glumly, then said something which made Tom shake his head.

'He said that if he and Maria lived here with me they could help pick the fruit.'

He said something in Spanish to Juan which produced a response, followed by more emphatic head-shaking from Tom. He looked a little embarrassed.

'He says that if I married you, you could look after them,' he murmured.

Tessa found herself blushing.

'I've told them we'll go after an early lunch,' Tom continued. 'That will give us time to calm them down and get them to understand that I haven't any choice.' He nodded at the window, where heavy raindrops were now hitting the small panes of glass. 'I just hope the roads don't get flooded.'

As he spoke, Juan whispered something to Maria and the children scrambled to their feet and made for the staircase. Tom's eyes followed them.

'They can cuddle up on the bed and tell each other what a horrible man I am,' he said wryly.

'As you said, you have no choice,' Tessa said gently.

'But I can't feel happy about the situation. If only their father would reappear as suddenly as he vanished! I did put a note in the tent saying where they are.'

Lunch was to be tortilla, the popular Spanish egg and potato omelette. It was prepared by the light of oil lamps as the rain grew heavier and daylight almost vanished. Tessa managed to find a miscellaneous collection of crockery and cutlery and laid it out on the heavy wooden table in the living room. When Tom said the food was ready she went to the foot of the stairs.

'Juan! Maria!' she called.

There was no response. She mounted a few steps before calling again. 'Juan! Maria!'

Silence. Perhaps they had fallen asleep. She would have to wake them up. She climbed the rest of the stairs and gently opened the bedroom door. The blankets on the great bed were crumpled, but no children lay cuddled in them. She looked round. The room was empty but the window was open and rain was driving in, soaking the curtains and the rug on the floor. Tessa rushed to the window and looked out, but could see nothing but the trees and the rain. She closed the window and stumbled hastily down the stairs.

'Tom! They've gone! The children have run away!'

Tom dropped the pan he was holding and raced up the stairs to see for himself, as if he was unable to accept what she said. He came down slowly, step by step, and opened the front door.

The rain and wind invaded the cosy little room.

'They're out there somewhere,' he said heavily, 'trying to run away from us. But they'll never survive in this weather.' His voice became urgent. 'I've got to look for them!'

He was about to plunge outside when Tessa caught his arm.

'You need a raincoat, and find one for me too.'

He did not try to dissuade her, but instead seized two old jackets from hooks beside the door and tossed one to her. Then, together, they faced the storm. It was at its height and Tessa found it difficult to stand against the force of the wind which lashed the fruit trees, making it almost impossible to hear anything except the noise of the wind through the branches. Leaves torn from the trees whipped their faces. Heads bent, the two of them trudged forward, calling out the names of the children, stopping from time to time to listen for a response. But even if there had been one they could not have heard it, and after half an hour or so Tom stopped.

'This is hopeless!' he shouted in Tessa's ear. She nodded despondently.

Tom made one last effort. Taking a deep breath, he cupped his mouth in his hands and shouted as loudly as he could. Then they stood and listened, but all they could hear was the scream of the wind through the trees. Tessa had a sudden vision of the two children, helpless in this storm, gradually growing weaker and succumbing to fatigue, sinking to the ground. Suddenly tears were streaming down her cheeks and she was sobbing. Tom had been scanning the trees, but now he took a step towards her and put his arms round her awkwardly.

'We'll find them somehow,' he promised. But the storm's intensity seemed to be increasing and finally they struggled back to the house, defeated.

'I'll have to call the police and hope that somehow they can arrange a search party,' Tom said, but when he tried his mobile phone his face tightened and he threw it down angrily. 'No signal,' he told Tessa. 'This storm must be affecting reception.' He sank down on a chair and put his head in his hands. 'This is all my fault. I should have taken the two of them to town yesterday afternoon, or this morning at the latest. If anything happens to them, I'll never forgive myself.'

There was nothing she could say to comfort him and they sat in silence, imagining what was happening to the two lost children, desperately trying to think how they could get help. Then, suddenly, Tessa's head lifted. She thought she heard a noise at the front door. Tom had heard it as well.

'It's probably a branch blown against the door,' he guessed.

'It sounds like an animal scratching,' Tessa said doubtfully, wondering what wild beast could have been driven out of the woods by the wind and rain.

The scratching came again, and Tom

stood up and opened the door a crack so that the rain could not drive in. Then suddenly he recklessly threw the door wide open and stooped to embrace the huddled heap on the doorstep. In a second Tessa was beside him and together they lifted the two children into the shelter of the room and then slammed the door shut.

Juan was holding Maria tightly in his arms. He tried to speak, but his teeth were chattering with cold and they could not make out the words, while his sister was virtually unconscious.

Gently Tessa and Tom persuaded the boy to release his sister from his protective grasp. Both children were soaking wet, shivering still in spite of the warm room. Together Tom and Tessa rapidly stripped the children of their T-shirts and jeans and briskly rubbed them dry with bath towels in spite of their protesting yelps, eager to get the blood circulating properly again. Then the two were wrapped in some old blankets which Tom produced. By this time both the children had partly revived, and, sitting in front of the wood stove, Juan and Maria gratefully drank mugs of hot milk and then complained of their hunger. They were soon eating heartily and even managed to devour the cold tortilla which had been abandoned at lunchtime. Finally, unable to eat any more, the children sank back in their chairs, Maria's head drooping with weariness. Juan lifted his head and said something.

'He said that they were going to look for their father,' Tom translated to Tessa, 'but then the rain came, Maria couldn't go any further, and this was the only place he knew where he could bring her to keep her safe.' He ruffled the boy's hair. 'Thank goodness he did.' He added something in Spanish and the boy blushed and looked gratified.

5

The children had survived their ordeal and were recovering rapidly, but the problem of what was to happen to them still remained. After a while Tom pulled a chair close to the children and started some earnest discussion with Juan. Tessa could only wait to be told what was being said. The boy protested at first, but finally, with obvious reluctance, he nodded. Tom turned to Tessa.

'We've agreed to some kind of compromise,' he told her. 'As it's getting late the children will stay here tonight and we'll go into town tomorrow and ask around, show people the photograph of their father and ask if they have seen him. He was called Joaquin, by the way. If we can't find any trace of him, then Juan has agreed that we will have to go to the police.'

'I think they are very lucky children.

You're going to a great deal of trouble for them,' she told him, and was rewarded by his smile.

'They have you to thank as well. You came with me to look for them in spite of the storm, and I'd have found it difficult to look after both of them without you.'

Moved, she avoided his eyes and looked at her watch. 'It's time I was going,' she said, looking out of the window. The rain and wind seemed to have subsided slightly. 'Can I have another lift? I think it would be safer to take the children with us again, even though I'm sure after their experience they wouldn't try to run away again.'

'I'll just check the road.'

Tom went out and returned ten minutes later, shaking his head despondently.

'It's bad news. I can't get the van out tonight. The path is a sea of mud and the van would get stuck before we made it round the first bend.'

She stared at him, appalled.

'So what can I do? I'll have to walk!'
He laughed mirthlessly.

'Not a good idea. The paths are inches deep in water and the wind has blown some trees down. It's going to be a full house here tonight because I'm afraid you'll have to stay here as well.'

'No! I must be able to get back to the hotel somehow!'

'Go and look for yourself.'

Finally, reluctantly, after she had been outside and seen the terrible condition of the road for herself, she had to accept that there was no safe way she could get back to the shelter and comfort of the hotel that night.

'That double bed will hold the children again,' Tom said. 'You can have the camp bed and I'll sleep on the couch down here.'

There was still the problem of letting Diane know what had happened to her friend, but a little later Tom tried his mobile again, and this time it worked, so Tessa used it to call the hotel and asked to speak to Diane.

'One moment,' said the hotel receptionist. 'I think I can see her in the lobby.' There was an interval of indistinct murmurs and then Diane's voice.

'Hello? Is that you, Tessa? What's happened? Where on earth are you? You were supposed to be back about lunch time.'

'Rain has happened,' Tessa said bitterly. 'The roads are impassable, so I'll have to stay here at the farm for the night.'

There was a short silence before Diane spoke again, and Tessa could hear the speculation in her friend's voice.

'So the two of you are staying there — you and Tom Collins?'

'The two of us, with two children as chaperones.'

'I thought you were getting rid of them today?'

'Things did not go according to plan.'

'Oh! What time will you be back tomorrow?'

'That depends on the road and the rain, and possibly on the children. Expect me when you see me.'

There was a pause, more indistinct noises, before she heard Diane saying coldly, 'Do you mind?' then Diane was speaking to her again.

'I'm sorry about that,' her friend said. 'That Spaniard who tried to pick us up the other night has been chatting up the receptionist and then seemed to be trying to listen in to our call. Well, the best of luck, Tessa, and you can tell me everything when you get back — and I mean everything!'

Tessa sighed as she ended the call, imagining Diane's relentless interrogation when she finally got back to the hotel.

There was not much food left in Tom's store cupboard after he had concocted a supper for the four of them of eggs with the addition of whatever scraps remained.

'I'd better go shopping some time tomorrow,' he commented. 'It's going to be a busy day. I've promised to do an afternoon's work at a house that is being renovated, so I'll have the morning to see what I can do about the children and then find time to buy myself some food.'

'That's if the van can get through the roads,' Tessa reminded him nervously. 'Didn't you say you were stuck here for three days once?'

'Don't!' He peered out the window and seemed pleased by what he saw. 'The rain has stopped, and it doesn't take long for the water to drain away, so we shouldn't be trapped here tomorrow. With a little bit of luck, the worst should be gone by morning.'

The words were encouraging, but his expression wasn't too hopeful. Tessa stared out at the dark, wet trees, and her heart sank. She should have stayed at the hotel and left Tom to deal with the children. They were nothing to do with her. It was all Diane's fault. If she hadn't gone off with Matt and left Tessa to amuse herself she would never have met Tom.

Maria and Juan were exhausted by their experiences and did not object to going to bed early, though both were a little bad-tempered, obviously fretting about what the next day would bring. Tessa discovered they had slept in their underclothes the previous night after a quick cursory wash, but she found their nightclothes and wash bags in the holdalls from their tent and insisted on a thorough wash. After she had supervised their toilet they snuggled down together in the great bed happily enough. Maria lifted her sleepy face for a goodnight kiss, and Tessa touched her forehead with her lips, a lump rising in her throat. Who would be looking after this little girl this time tomorrow? Would anyone kiss her good-night?

Tom had cleared the dishes and was washing up when she went downstairs, She sank down on the battered couch and watched his quietly efficient movements by the glow of the oil lamps.

When he had finished he dried his hands and then opened a cupboard and lifted out a laptop computer which he placed on the table.

'I have to keep checking my emails,' he explained. 'Sometimes people want a job done in a hurry.'

An idea occurred to Tessa as he was jotting down a few notes.

'If you've got access to the internet, would you mind looking something up for me?'

'No trouble. Is it a site or a name?'

'It's the man you met at the hotel — Matt Dixon. He and my friend Diane are getting very close, but there are one or two things about him which have puzzled me. Of course,' she added hurriedly, 'there may be nothing about him, but he does work with computers himself, so his name may be mentioned.'

Tom's eyes were on the screen as he busily tapped away, then he stopped to read what had appeared before tapping again.

x

136

'There are a few references to a Matt Dixon. Apparently he designs programmes for financial organisations. It sounds like heavy stuff.' He was still watching the screen. 'There are quite a lot of references to a Matthew Dixon.' He stabbed at the keyboard. 'Wait! There's an article here about Matthew Dixon which says he had a son called Matt, and there's a picture. Come and see.'

The photograph showed a middle-aged man with his arm round a black-haired boy who did look rather like a young Matt. The picture illustrated a story about an old manor house with a large garden which Matthew Dixon had bought. Apparently both house and garden had been neglected for some time, and Matthew had intended to bring both of them back into good repair and the article said that he had fulfilled this intention. There was a smaller picture of a large house built in red brick, and Tessa saw that there were some big beech trees near the house.

'Is that your man?'

'Very possibly, but I'd have to check with him.'

Frowning with concentration, Tom pressed some more keys.

'Here's something at the end of the article! Didn't you say his house had been damaged by a tree?'

This time he had found a quotation from a newspaper giving details of the damage recently suffered by the ancient house when a tree had blown down on it.

'Thank you, Tom. That definitely clinches it.'

Tom was still looking at the screen.

'I thought I'd taken on a big job when I bought this house, but I hate to think how much it would cost to do up a manor house like that. Either this Matt Dixon is very rich and can afford the repairs, or he's penniless because it's taken all his cash.'

Tessa sat down again. A penniless man wouldn't be living in a four-star hotel. If Diane's Matt was the owner of the house and garden shown, he must be a wealthy man and would have had no difficulty in buying her a genuine sapphire ring.

Tom put his computer away and from the same cupboard proudly produced a bottle of wine.

'It's pretty basic,' he warned her, 'but I think we've earned a drink.'

It was not as bad as he suggested, and they sipped steadily, finding it ever easier to talk to each other. Talking about his travels again, Tom described some of the longer trips he had taken. It was clear that occasionally he had been away from England for over a year at a time even before he settled in Spain.

'Didn't you miss your home and your family,' Tessa enquired.

'Not really. My parents went through a rough patch when I was a teenager, and I think I started travelling to get away from the trouble and the recriminations.'

He was a pleasant man, good

company, and others must have seen this, before and after Lucia.

'Did you always travel by yourself before you met Lucia?' she probed delicately.

He smiled and shrugged.

'Most of the time. Occasionally I paired off with someone else for a while, but it never lasted. With the exception of Lucia, I've always liked to be on my own.'

'I know how you feel. I often feel the same,' she said hastily.

'This certainly isn't the holiday you were expecting,' he remarked, looking at the dark windows. 'First your friend is spending most of her time with this man she's met, and then I virtually kidnap you and make you look after two strange children.'

'I don't mind. It's more interesting than just sitting in the hotel dodging Pedro Valdes and I'm happy for Diane.'

There was a silence. She was dozing, her head resting against his shoulder. He shifted gently and put his arm round her to support her. She turned her head muzzily and looked up at him. Their faces were inches apart and they looked at each other for the space of a long-drawn out breath, and then he bent his head and kissed her. She found herself responding with sudden urgency, and soon their bodies were pressed together. His hand slid under her T-shirt and moved up to clasp her breast and in turn she found her hands were inside his shirt, stroking the satin-smooth skin at the side of his body. His other hand slid to the waistband of her jeans. She tensed, then relaxed, and at that moment there was a wail from upstairs. They jerked apart guiltily.

'It's Maria. I'll see what's the matter,' Tessa said hoarsely, and then managed to heave her reluctant body upright and make for the stairs on unsteady feet. While Juan slept steadily on, Maria was demanding comfort in these strange surroundings. Tessa held her and soothed her, stroking her dark hair and crooning to her gently until the child's eyes closed in sleep again.

She went downstairs very slowly.

'I think it's time I joined them,' she said awkwardly to Tom, who nodded stiffly, not meeting her eyes.

Soon she was in the camp bed in the room next to the two sleeping children, wearing an old shirt of Tom's which he had offered her earlier as an improvised nightdress. In spite of her fatigue it took her quite a while to get to sleep. What had she been thinking of, almost offering herself to a man she barely knew? The intimacy of their situation and the wine scarcely seemed enough explanation. She would leave him the next day as soon as the problem of the children was settled, and she would take care not to see him again. But Tessa was still keenly aware of the way her body had responded instinctively to his nearness. She had never felt like that before with Eric Lester or any of her few previous boyfriends, and had privately decided that sex did not mean a great deal to her. Now she realised that she might have been wrong, that she had simply not met a man before who could awaken her physically. Why did it have to be Tom Collins, a man who was definitely not her type, who was probably still in love with his dead girl friend, and whom she would never see after the holiday ended?

The next morning the children were already awake and running up and down the stairs when she woke, and their demands for food, answered by instructions to wash and dress before they ate, gave no chance for embarrassment when a yawning, tousled Tom threw off the blankets covering him on the couch and greeted her. Once again, Tessa supervised the children while they washed and dressed, and she did her best to comb Maria's hair in spite of the little girl's reluctance to keep still.

The sun blazed from a cloudless sky, and Tom made a brief excursion outside and came back very relieved to report that the dirt road was passable. Breakfast over and the dishes washed, the four of them made their way to the van, carrying the two holdalls containing Juan and Maria's worldly goods and the envelope full of documents, ready to be passed to their next temporary guardians. In spite of managing a quick wash, Tessa felt stale and dirty, her hair unbrushed and roughly straightened with Tom's small comb. Searching for the children in the storm and then bathing them had made yesterday's clothes look very tired and creased. The children were fretful, wondering what their future would be, and there was still a residual awkwardness between her and Tom. Still, soon it would all be over. He would drive her back to the hotel and then carry on to town with the children.

Tom stood with his hands on his hips and sighed as he saw Juan moodily kicking one of the van's tyres. He spoke sharply, and the boy slouched away, head hanging down.

'I'm going to have trouble managing these two,' Tom murmured. 'They're not in a cooperative mood today.'

'They're worried because they don't know what is going to happen to them,' Tessa pointed out unnecessarily.

'I know that,' he snapped, then gave an apologetic shrug. 'But I don't know either. I just know that they can't stay here.' He managed a grin. 'Well, it's not your affair. Get in the van and I'll take you back to your comfortable four-star hotel and you can forget all about the three of us.'

Suddenly, to her own surprise, Tessa shook her head vigorously.

'No. I'm as involved with these two as you are. I'll come to town and look after the children while you ask the shopkeepers and businessmen if they have seen the father. That's if you'd like me to come,' she added hastily.

His face showed his relief.

'Please! I didn't dare ask you, because I've caused you so much trouble already. After all, as I said, this

145

is not the comfortable holiday you paid for, but I should be very grateful if you would help me for just a couple of hours more. I promise I'll get you back to the hotel then.'

So all four of them crowded into the little van, the children torn between fear of the unknown and the feeling that they were setting out on a great adventure. When he started the engine and put it into gear, the wheels spun in the mud, but then gripped the path and the van moved forward with Tom carefully negotiating a route round the remaining pools of water. They were soon nearing the town.

They started by questioning shop-keepers near the centre, but with no success, so they moved on to a small trading estate on the edge of town as it was possible that the children's father could have tried to find work there. One or two people looked at the photograph and thought that Joaquin might have been one of the men who had called recently seeking work, only to be told there was none available, but there were many men looking for work now and they could not be sure.

'At least we know that if it was him he was trying to find work, not just deserting the children and running away,' Tom commented after they had talked to one man.

'But where did he go from here?'

Tom scowled.

'Where do we go? If he did get in trouble then the police will know, but there is one more place we can try before we decide it's hopeless and take the children to the police station.'

He drove through some narrow streets to a building, little more than a hut, with a sign outside announcing that the proprietor repaired all kinds of woodwork. The only person there was an elderly man who spoke passable English and who greeted Tom as an old friend. He seemed to welcome their interruption but looked very vague when shown the photograph of Joaquin.

'He looks like thousands of other

men,' he pointed out. 'You say the photo was taken some time ago? So he's changed now, anyway.' He took another look and seemed to hesitate. 'I suppose he could have been . . . '

'You may have seen him? Even if you're not sure, tell us about it. It may help,' Tom said urgently.

The man looked at the children in the van while thoughtfully rubbing his bald patch.

'You are looking for their father? Well, if it was him I saw, then I'm afraid this is bad news. Somebody who looked rather like him called here a couple of days ago asking if I could give him some work — any work — even if it was for only a few hours. I had to say no, and I remember how sad and downcast he looked as he walked away. He wasn't looking where he was going.' He paused. 'Then a van came round that corner, far too fast of course, and it hit him before he had a chance to dodge.'

Tessa gasped and Tom leaned forward urgently.

'What happened to him?'

'The van stopped and the driver got out to look at him, shouting that it was his own fault because he wasn't looking out for traffic. I rushed in here and called for an ambulance. Then I heard an engine start up and when I came out the van and its driver were gone, leaving the poor man lying on the ground. Fortunately the ambulance came within minutes and took him away.'

'How badly was he hurt?'

The man shook his head.

'I don't know. I didn't dare move him in case I made things worse.' He looked up sharply. 'But he wasn't dead, if that's what you're afraid of. I saw him move an arm.'

Tessa and Tom thanked him and moved away a little to confer before returning to the children.

'Where would the ambulance take him? Is there a hospital in the town?' Tessa asked.

'There is a kind of hospital,' Tom told her. 'It's very small, and really it's just used for holding clinics, but it does deal with accidents. He was probably taken there first to see how badly he was hurt, and they'll know where he is if he was moved on somewhere else or they'll tell us if he was just given first aid and then released.'

They returned to the van and tried to prepare the children for their next call, Tom telling them that a doctor might be looking after their father for a while, but they were going to find out whether this was true or not. The children seemed to sense their apprehension and their faces grew pinched and pale and Juan took Maria's hand.

The hospital was a white one-storey building. Tom found a parking space in front of it, got out and went round to help Tessa out.

'I don't know whether to hope their father's here or not,' he murmured, looking at the children. 'If he is, or if he's been badly hurt and sent elsewhere, we'll just have a whole new set of problems to deal with.'

'At least I hope we can find out something,' she returned. 'Not knowing what has happened is worse than anything.'

Just at that moment an open sports car drove slowly past them. Tessa recognised it and saw Pedro Valdes in the driving seat and turned away, hoping he had not seen her. She stood uncertainly next to Tom for a few seconds before he squared his shoulders and took a deep breath.

'Well, let's see what they can tell us.'

They made the children promise to sit still and not touch anything, and then went into the building to make their enquiries. A hospital receptionist greeted them but they soon found that she had no record of a Joaquin Diaz being treated there.

'He may have been brought here because he was the victim of a traffic accident a few days ago. Please, look at the photograph again,' Tom urged.

She took a quick look, leafed through some documents, and then called a passing nurse and showed her the photograph. The nurse shrugged, frowning, and then suddenly turned excitedly to the receptionist. There was a rapid exchange between the two while Tom listened attentively.

'She thinks it looks a little like a man who was brought in a couple of days ago after he'd been knocked down. Of course, if it was the children's father he would look very different after the accident. She says his leg had been hurt and they dealt with that. But they don't know his name because apparently he was knocked unconscious in the accident and since then he seems to have lost his memory. They've kept him here because he wasn't badly injured enough physically to need treatment at a bigger hospital, and they have been hoping that his memory would return after a good rest. But they are planning to send him to a bigger hospital this afternoon if he still can't remember anything.'

'Can we see him? It might be the man we're looking for, and we've tried everywhere else.'

The nurse seemed reluctant to agree but Tom persevered, appealing to her with the sad story of the two children, till in the end she relented and nodded slowly, but there was still a problem.

'Even if we think he looks like the man in the photograph, we certainly couldn't positively identify him just from this so I suppose we will have to get the children to take a look. I'll ask if the staff are prepared to allow that.'

Tom went to fetch Juan and Maria. He came back, holding a child by each hand. They looked very serious.

'I've told them we're all going to have a look at this man,' Tom explained. 'I've also told them they've got to be very quiet, and just nod or shake their heads to show if they know him or not.'

He looked at the children sternly and they looked back at him with big eyes and nodded to show that they were going to do as they were told.

The nurse, having received a doctor's

consent, led them through the corridors. There were windows through which one could look into some of the rooms and she stopped at one and indicated that Tom and Tessa should look. They saw a room with two beds, only one of which was occupied. On it lay a dark-haired man whose right leg was bare to the knee and heavily bandaged. He was sleeping, but very restlessly, his arms twitching, his head turning from side to side. The nurse murmured something and shrugged her shoulders as if she had little hope that the patient had improved.

There was an impatient tug at Tessa's hand. She looked down at Maria, who was giving little jumps up and down and she realised that the corridor window was too high for either of the children to look through. She pointed this out, and the nurse, with obvious reluctance, quietly opened the door a little so that the children could peer in at the sleeping man.

Suddenly the quiet of the hospital

was broken by a shrill scream.

'Papa!' Maria pushed past the nurse and hurtled into the room. 'Papa! Papa!'

Juan followed her, his face shining, and he seized the sleeping man by one arm, shaking it to wake him up.

'Well, we've found their father,' Tom commented, stating the obvious, 'but what happens now?'

What happened was that the man on the bed opened his eyes and looked round, dazed, as though he was waking from a long, deep sleep. Then he saw Juan and Maria and tried to sit up, only to fall back on his pillows, his arms stretched out towards them. Now the nurse was in the room, trying to shoo the children out so she could deal with the patient, but they flatly refused to move, clinging to their father with radiant faces. As Tessa and Tom tried to help the nurse, a white-coated doctor appeared and started issuing loud orders. After a few minutes of confusion, Tom and Tessa managed to get the children out of the ward and into a waiting-room by telling them that the doctor had to look at their father and by promising that they would soon be allowed to return to his bedside. In fact it was half an hour later when the nurse came to fetch the children and take them back to him and by then the children had begun complaining about the delay ever more loudly and Tom had begun to fidget and look at his watch.

'He is asking for you,' the nurse told the children, who did not wait for Tom and Tessa but dashed past her down the corridor.

When Tom and Tessa reached the room, Joaquin Diaz was sitting up on the bed, his arms around his children, all three radiant with happiness, Juan talking non-stop, until Joaquin bade his son be quiet and in his turn poured out a flood of Spanish. Tom shook his head and replied in the same language.

'Juan has told him what has been happening to them and he is thanking us for taking care of the children,' he translated. 'He says they might have died in the woods without us. I told him we only did what anybody would have done, that we couldn't just leave them there to fend for themselves.'

'What happens next?'

'What happens next is that I've got to get to work. I'm glad we've reunited them with their father, but I've still got to earn a living,' Tom said firmly. 'I'll bring in the two holdalls.'

Soon it had been agreed with the nurses that the children would be allowed to stay with their father, providing they were reasonably quiet. As he was threatening to rise from his bed and walk off with them otherwise, there had been little choice. Various tests would be carried out on Joaquin that afternoon, and the results would decide what action the doctors thought necessary.

Tom and Tessa found they were no longer needed and could go. Almost reluctantly, they said goodbye to the children, shook hands with their father, and walked out of the room, it was difficult to realise that they had now been freed from responsibility.

'What happens to the children if their father has to stay in hospital after all?' Tessa wondered as they made their way out. 'Even if it is decided that he is fit enough to leave hospital, that bad leg means he can't go back to that little tent with the children. He hasn't any money and he hasn't got a job either.'

'That's not our problem any longer,' Tom said tersely. 'I'm late for my next job, and if the customer is upset I'll have enough problems of my own to worry about.' He looked at her concerned face and gave a wry grin. 'Don't worry. I do care what happens to them and I'll probably find out. I told him I would call back at the hospital after I finished work so that I could explain to him properly what has been happening to his children during the past couple of days.'

He stopped suddenly on the steps of

the hospital, staring at his van.

'What the hell . . . ?'

The van was sagging to one side. Tom went down the steps hastily and she saw him go round the vehicle, bending to check it. He returned to her grim-faced.

'Two of the tyres are flat.'

'Oh! Do you think that happened when we were driving through the trees? The rain must have washed sharp stones on to the road and some might have got at the tyres.'

He shook his head.

'This isn't accidental damage. Both tyres have been slashed more than once with a knife.' Hands on hips, he stared around. 'Some idiot, probably drunk, thought it was a big joke to do this, I suppose.'

Tessa thought of Pedro Valdes driving past, but surely even he wouldn't do anything so mean and petty, would he?

'What can you do?'

'If it was one tyre, I've got a spare, but as it's two I'll have to contact a garage.' She heard him swear under his breath. 'And I'll have to contact the man I'm working for as well and tell him I'll be late. He won't be pleased.'

Tessa suddenly thought of her own situation.

'I'm not sure what to do . . . ,' she began, but Tom wasn't listening, instead he was busy waving down a passing taxi. He spoke to the driver and handed him some notes before turning to Tessa.

'There's nothing you can do here, so this driver will take you back to your hotel.' He held the door open for her, glancing at his watch yet again. Unwilling to delay him any more, Tessa got in the taxi. She wanted to ask him to let her know what he found out at the hospital later, but he had shut the taxi door firmly. Then something apparently occurred to him and he rapped urgently on the window, which she lowered quickly.

'Thank you for all your help,' was all

he said before stepping back and waving the driver off. Tessa twisted to watch him until the taxi turned a corner and he disappeared from sight. So that was that. The little family had been reunited, her services were no longer required and Tom was free to return to his solitary life. End of story.

6

At the hotel she squared her shoulders and walked into the reception area, trying to ignore the stares of the guests leaving the dining room after lunch as they saw her straggly hair and her clothes, reduced to crumpled weckage by two days' wear and the previous afternoon's exposure to the storm. Tessa was also becoming aware of hunger pangs. It had been a long time since breakfast, but she did not think the restaurant would welcome her in her present state. While she was wondering what to do, Pedro Valdes walked by, saw her, and looked at her with exaggerated surprise before making a mock bow.

'Your plumber boy-friend does not seem to treat you very well,' he sneered. 'I noticed he didn't even bring you back himself. What was the matter? Trouble with his little white van?'

He laughed and walked off before she could say anything. She fumed. He must be guilty of maliciously slashing Tom's tyres, but she would never be able to prove it.

Looking down at her clothes, she decided she needed a wash even more urgently than food and made for the lifts. Diane was not in their room and Tessa stripped and took a long, hot shower, sank down on her bed, and fell fast asleep. She woke with a jump to find Diane gently shaking her awake.

'Tessa, what's been happening? Where have you been all this time? I've been worried sick!'

'I told you what had happened,' Tessa said groggily.

'Yes, but it was a bit lacking in detail, wasn't it, and I expected you back hours ago! I assumed you were still with Tom Collins, but I didn't know how to contact him and Matt and I aren't even sure exactly where his house is.'

Tessa propped herself up on her elbow.

'You guessed right. I was with Tom Collins at his house and in the town — and before you say anything, I was also with the two children I told you about.'

Diane sank down beside her friend.

'Oh. Then can I assume it was not the night of mad passion I thought it might be?'

'Certainly not! I had to stay there because the rain made the road impassable. We were lucky to get out this morning'

'Really? So you could have got back this morning? I notice you didn't hurry back here.'

'I was driving round town trying to find anyone who might recognise a photo of a man taken some years ago.' She explained what had happened. 'So you see, the children are back with their father, Tom Collins has got his house to himself, and I will never see any of them again! I'm going to stay in the hotel, have frequent hot showers, sunbathe when it's possible, and be first in the queue for meals I haven't prepared. So that's my story.' She looked at Diane. 'And how have you been getting on in my absence?'

Her friend was smiling, dreamy-eyed.

'It's been marvellous. Matt and I have really been happy together.'

'Really? Together? So you took full advantage of my absence?'

Diane was blushing.

'Let's just say I didn't spend a lonely night.'

Tessa sat up and hugged her knees.

'So it's serious. Is this going to be more than a holiday romance after all?'

Diane shook her head decisively.

'No. I've told Matt my rules. We can have a great time while the holiday lasts, but then I fly home and he will never hear from me again.'

'And does he accept that?'

'He has no choice.'

Had Matt accepted that without a fight or had he argued? Diane was obviously not going to tell her. Tessa swung her legs off the bed, wondering whether she should tell Diane what Tom had found out on the internet about Matt, but she wanted to have a word with Matt first if that were possible. She could not understand why Matt had told Diane so little about himself. Why was he so secretive about his big house?

'Well, stand aside. I'm going to dress and make up very carefully, and then I'm going to enjoy a long dinner with quite a bit of wine.'

Which she did, managing to ignore most of the whispered comments about her overnight absence and less than smart reappearance which seemed to be the main topic of conversation among the elderly clientele.

'Ignore them,' Matt murmured, as they heard a louder than usual comment. 'The poor dears are desperate for a bit of gossip. They should be grateful to you.'

'Well, we'll see you have a good day tomorrow, Tessa,' Diane assured her friend.

166

Matt looked guilty.

'Not me, I'm afraid. I'm going to be busy with my computer for most of tomorrow. I've got to finish this project as soon as I can. I'm already late.' He looked at Diane's disappointed face. 'I'm sorry. I've been neglecting my work to be with you, but I can't put it off any longer.'

'Don't you get tired of sitting in your room with a computer?' Tessa asked hastily, before Diane could say anything.

'It's a living. Anyway, I'll have to go to Granada soon for a face-to-face discussion with a client who may offer me a very nice contract.' He ran his fingers through his mop of black curls. 'That means I'll have to dig out my suit and get my hair cut, so as to look like a proper businessman.' He turned to Diane. 'I'm really sorry about tomorrow, sweetheart, but at least Tessa will be here to keep you company.'

Diane took a deep breath, then seemed resigned to accepting the inevitable. She had remembered something.

'We booked to go on an excursion up into the hills tomorrow. Tessa, you can have Matt's place. We'll enjoy a pleasant trip while he stays here hunched over his computer.'

Tessa was glad to agree to this. It was the kind of thing she had been hoping to do this holiday, and Matt looked very relieved. At least a day spent sight-seeing would stop her wondering what had happened when Tom went back to the hospital, and what had been arranged for Joaquin and his children.

At one point in the evening Diane excused herself for a few minutes and Tessa seized the opportunity her absence provided.

'Matt, Tom and I were looking people up on the internet yesterday evening, and we did put your name in.'

Matt looked at her warily.

'Really? Did you find anything?'

'We found a picture of the old manor

house and garden that your father bought.'

He bit his lip.

'So?'

'So Diane doesn't seem to know that she is going out with a rich landowner.'

He held up a hand.

'Hold on! I may have an Elizabethan house with big grounds, but that doesn't mean I'm rich. They cost a lot to maintain, even when trees aren't falling over.'

'But you're not hard up. You can afford to maintain them?'

'True,' He leant forward earnestly. 'Look, Tessa, I gather you haven't told Diane about this. Please leave it to me. Diane says she won't see me again after the holiday is over. So until I can persuade her in other ways to go on seeing me I'm not going to tell her that I've got this big, impressive house, in case she thinks I'm hinting that she should stay in touch because I have money, and I can imagine how furiously she would react to that.'

'So you do want to go on seeing her?'

'Of course I do!' Matt said warmly.

Tessa thought quickly.

'Then I won't tell her,' she decided, and Matt sat back in relief just as Diane returned.

'What have the pair of you been talking about?' she asked, looking at them suspiciously.

'Nothing interesting,' Tessa said airily. 'I was just asking Matt if he knew where I could find a rich boyfriend.'

The excursion into the hills the next day was not just a pleasant distraction, it was absorbing. The Alpujarras range of hills soared up a short distance inland and the day was spent driving along narrow, twisting roads which climbed up to small white villages and opened up immense vistas of wild landscape. One pretty white-washed village apparently had an astonishingly high number of British residents.

'You could live here very happily, and

you wouldn't even have to learn Spanish,' marvelled a fellow excursionist.

'Then why bother to come to Spain?'

The woman spread her arms wide and looked up at the blue sky.

'For the sunshine.'

Was that enough? Tom liked the sunshine, but he had also found work and friends, and restoring his house had given him a purpose. He belonged here now as much as any of his Spanish neighbours. It was his home. She frowned as this thought occurred to her. She had to forget Tom Collins.

They returned to the hotel just before five o'clock. As she collected her key from Reception, Tessa was given a scribbled message. It said someone had called her from a number which she recognised as the number on Tom's van. He must have realised that she would want to know what had happened to the little family. It also meant that he had not decided to cut all contact with her completely as soon as she had been driven out of sight in the taxi.

She called the number as soon as she got to her room, but there was no answer. She tried a couple of times more, but it was six o'clock before there was a reply. When she heard Tom's voice she found herself gripping the receiver tightly.

'Tessa? Good. Your receptionist wasn't sure what time you would be back and I've just come in myself. Listen, would you like to come over here for dinner tonight? I know it's short notice, so I'll understand if you can't.'

Her heart thumped. The invitation was a little half-hearted, but he actually wanted to see her, even though he no longer needed her help with the children!

He went on.

'It's Joaquin. He wants to thank you for what you did for Maria and Juan.'

She nearly dropped the phone.

'They're with you at the farm — all three of them?'

172

She heard him laugh.

'I'm afraid so. I'll understand if you never want to see this place again, but Joaquin keeps insisting that he wants to thank you in person.'

It dawned rather depressingly on Tessa then that it was Joaquin, the children's father, and not Tom, who was responsible for the invitation.

'I don't think I can make it,' she said coldly. 'I've been out all day and there's a show on at the hotel this evening.'

She heard an exasperated sigh.

'Then I'll have to pile them all in the van tomorrow and bring him to see you or he won't stop pestering me.'

Her eyes widened in horror. The little old ladies were gossiping enough about her now. What other lurid stories would they conjure up if a van full of children and young men arrived at the hotel demanding to see her?

'No, don't do that! I'll come. What time will you pick me up?'

There was a short silence.

'Actually, Tessa, would you mind

getting a taxi here about eight o'clock? I'll pay when it gets here, but Joaquin is a comparative stranger and I don't want to leave him at the farm without me.'

She gritted her teeth, almost announced that she couldn't come after all, but then reluctantly agreed to do as he asked.

She went to tell Diane of the arrangement for the evening. Her friend was not at all pleased. Matt had not yet reappeared and Diane clearly felt very sorry for herself when she heard that her friend would not be there either, so she faced an evening by herself. The omens did not foretell a happy evening for either of them.

The taxi which the hotel summoned for her found the farm without trouble. Tom was waiting outside.

'Thank you for coming,' he said formally, after paying the driver.

'It was rather inconvenient,' Tessa said briefly.

They looked at each other uncertainly, and she knew that both of them were remembering that brief time in each other's arms, wondering what would have happened if Maria hadn't woken up. They started to walk towards the house without saying any more, keeping a little apart, but before they reached it the door suddenly burst open and Maria and Juan ran out to throw their arms around her, greeting her with kisses and hugs as if they had known her since they were born. She forgot her pride and dignity and knelt to embrace them. Then Joaquin appeared, limping and leaning on a stick but mobile, and poured out his thanks in Spanish, which was hastily translated by Tom. Tessa was touched by the transformation from the unconscious figure on the hospital bed to this demonstrative, alert man, obviously delighted to be reunited with his children. She asked Tom to tell Joaquin how pleased she had been to be able to help.

'Come and sit by the table,' Tom told her. 'Joaquin has insisted on taking over the cooking.' Soon she was seated. The children had disappeared into the house, following their father, but now they came out again, Maria carefully carrying a plate of appetizers and Juan holding two glasses of wine. Tom took the drinks and handed one to Tessa.

'While we're waiting for the meal to be ready, I'll tell you why they are here,' he said, sitting down with his own glass. 'You know I was going back to the hospital? Well, when I got there it was good news for Joaquin. The tests showed that his period of rest had healed the trauma of the accident. He still has to go back for a check-up in a week's time, but he was judged fit to leave the hospital. Just as well, because he was refusing to stay, insisting he had to take care of his children. The only trouble was that he had nowhere to go with them! As you said, he could hardly go back to live in that tiny tent with a bad leg. I brought the three of them back here to collect their tent and the few things the children had left here. On the way, Joaquin told me that he used to work in construction until the economic crisis meant so many jobs vanished. I had been a bit worried because I thought the job I had agreed to do might prove a bit too much for me to tackle by myself, and because of our search for Joaquin I didn't manage to finish it yesterday anyway. To cut a long story short, I let Joaquin and the children stay here last night and in return he came with me and helped me with the work this morning. Between us we did a good job and we've been asked to go back tomorrow to do something else.'

'And the children?'

He laughed.

'The man I am working for has six children, who were all running around the place, so he scarcely noticed an extra two, and Maria and Juan thoroughly enjoyed playing with other children.'

'What happens after tomorrow?'

He fidgeted uneasily.

'That's when the problems will start.

I haven't got anything more at present for him to help me with, and I'm not prepared to let him stay indefinitely here at the farm, and I think he understands that. Anyway, if he's to get a job and the children are to go to school he needs to be either in the town or near it. We'll see if anything turns up tomorrow.'

They were interrupted by the unexpected sound of a car approaching along the narrow road and Tom swivelled round, obviously surprised. Then he was on his feet, waving in greeting.

'Manuel! I wasn't expecting you but it's nice to see you.'

The man who got out of the slightly battered little car was in his forties, with a good-humoured face and a well-padded stomach.

'I hoped you could let me have some fruit,' he said cheerfully in English, then saw Tessa.

★ ★ ★

'Oh, no! Am I interrupting a pleasant evening with this young lady? Would you prefer I came another time?'

'It is a pleasant evening, but you're not interrupting. Tessa, this is Manuel. I told you about his restaurant and you have eaten his fruit tarts.'

At that moment Maria ran out of the house with Juan in hot pursuit, both giggling. Manuel looked at them in surprise, then turned enquiringly to Tom, who laughed.

'Come and see whether I've got what you need, and I'll explain everything.'

They disappeared into a stone shed, reappearing a few minutes later with boxes of fruit which they transferred to Manuel's car before Manuel returned to the table holding a couple of bottles of wine.

'I brought this as part payment for the fruit,' he explained to Tessa. 'Would you like to try it? It's much better than the awful stuff Tom usually drinks.'

Tom came back from a brief conversation with Joaquin to see her tasting the wine approvingly.

'Good,' he commented. 'You must stay for supper, Manuel, and then you can help us drink the rest of it.'

'Are you sure you have enough for me?'

'Joaquin is cooking enough for a dozen.'

At this Manuel settled himself happily on a bench and the three of them sat under the starlit sky, drinking the wine and chatting casually, with the occasional laughter of the children breaking the surrounding silence. Manuel was obviously interested in Tessa's hotel.

'I hear it's quite good,' he told her, 'and quite a lot of the clients come to my restaurant for lunch when they have been shopping or fancy a change of menu.' He smiled. 'If anybody asks you where they can get a good meal in town, tell them about my restaurant. They will not be disappointed.'

Finally Joaquin appeared in the doorway and announced that the meal was ready to be served. All six of them ate together companionably round the wooden table. There was a light salad to start with, and then a dish of chicken and spicy chorizo sausage, combined with vegetables and rice and rich with spices. Manuel breathed in the appetising odour, tasted it, and nodded his approval.

'Very good! Well cooked.' He repeated the compliment in Spanish, to Joaquin's obvious pleasure.

The chicken dish was succeeded by a platter of fruit and Joaquin went to make coffee.

'I suppose you don't have a vacancy for a cook, do you?' Tom asked in English, but Manuel shook his head.

'I'm afraid not, especially at this time of the year.'

'A pity. I just don't know what is going to happen to the three of them after tomorrow.'

After coffee Joaquin told the children to go indoors to get ready for bed. They were half-asleep already. Maria lifted her face to Tessa, who bent down and kissed her tenderly.

'Good-night, little one,' she said gently. 'I hope everything goes well for you.'

As the children went indoors, Manuel looked at his watch.

'It's been a very pleasant evening, but I'll have to leave you now,' he said regretfully. 'I left my daughter Sofia in charge of the restaurant but she'll want me there to help when we close up.' He looked at Tessa. 'Can I give you a lift back to the hotel, Tessa?'

There was a sharp movement from Tom, instantly stilled. Tessa waited a couple of seconds to see whether he would say anything to indicate that he would like her company for a little longer, but he was silent. She smiled at Manuel.

'I shall be most grateful for a lift. It will save Tom having to get that old van of his out.' She stood up, and Tom did the same, and she held out her hand to him. 'Thank you, Tom. I've enjoyed the evening and I've enjoyed Joaquin's cooking. I know you can't wait to be left alone in peace, so I hope he finds a job and somewhere to live soon.' She turned to Manuel. 'Shall we go? We don't want to keep your daughter waiting.'

She walked over to the car, followed by the two men. Tom opened the passenger door and she slid into the seat. The car smelt of fruit and spices.

'I suppose I won't see you again,' Tom said awkwardly. 'I wish I could tell you properly how grateful I am for your help, and how sorry I am for the way so much of your holiday has been spoilt.'

She smiled up at him.

'There's no need to be sorry. It's all been very interesting, and I've still got plenty of time for sunbathing and swimming.'

As Manuel switched on the ignition and drove off she waved at Tom, then sank back in her seat and sighed.

'You are sad to leave? You will see Tom again?' Manuel asked.

'I'm sad to leave. It is a lovely place.

But I don't expect to see Tom again.'

Of course she had thought that before.

They did not speak again until they drew up outside the hotel, where Manuel hurried round to open the car door for her.

'It has been a pleasure to meet you, Tessa. Perhaps I will see you at my restaurant before you go?'

'Perhaps,' she said, reluctant to commit herself. 'Thank you for the lift.'

She looked round the hotel lounge but could see neither Diane nor Matt, so she went up to her room. It was empty, and she had time to undress and shower before Diane came in. The two friends looked at each other.

'You first,' said Diane.

Tessa told her all about the evening.

'And you really don't expect to see this Tom again?' Diane queried, and Tessa shook her head.

'He has made it quite clear several times that he likes a quiet life by himself, and he doesn't need my help

184

any longer. He only asked me there this evening because Joaquin wanted to see me.'

'Would you like to see him again?' was Diane's next question.

Tessa thought about it.

'He had his good points,' she conceded, 'but he could be very irritating and I'm not going to bother my head about a man who isn't interested in me.'

'I suppose the poor man had one disadvantage from the start as far as you were concerned.'

'Meaning?'

'He's a tradesman — a plumber and electrician — so not your type. All your boyfriends have had white-collar jobs. There was the accountant and the financial adviser before the boring banker. From what you've said, I don't think your mother would welcome a plumber as your boyfriend either.'

Tessa sat bolt upright, eager to deny this allegation that she was a snob, but then slumped back. She had an uneasy feeling that there might be a grain of truth in it. She knew that Diane was certainly right about her mother's attitude.

'Nonsense!' she made herself say briskly. 'Now, how about you?'

Diane's lips curved in a slow smile.

'Matt appeared about twenty minutes after you left, full of apologies about neglecting me, and has been trying to make it up to me ever since.' Her smile widened. 'Very successfully, I may say.'

'But you're still going to say goodbye to him at the end of the holiday. Why on earth are you going to keep to your stupid rules when you like him so much?'

Diane's face grew serious. She looked away, avoiding Tessa's eyes.

'Romance doesn't last,' she said. 'My parents fell in love at first sight, got married as quickly as they could, and then found out after a short time that they were totally unsuited. They had different tastes, neither of them could manage money, they were completely disorganised.' She put her arm across her face. 'But by then my mother was expecting me, and they stayed together for my sake, as my mother kept telling me, but my childhood was a very unhappy one. Once my father couldn't take my mother's non-stop nagging any longer and I saw him hit her. Everybody, including me, was relieved when they finally split up. Do you realise that the word 'romantic' means 'a story, a lie'? It seems to me that romance is a delusion which means you can't see clearly what the other person is like. The more romance, the more likely it is that it will end badly. That is why I am not going to commit myself quickly to anyone, in case it all goes wrong. And even if I do finally get married, I'm going to be very practical. My future husband will have to have a steady job with a good income. Matt relies on contracts, on one-off jobs, and coming to Spain to stay in this good hotel while his house is repaired won't have been cheap.'

Tessa was regretting her promise to

Matt that she would keep quiet about his background,

'He seems to be doing well,' she argued. 'Probably he can afford to stay here.' She glanced pointedly at the ring on Diane's finger.

Diane ignored her.

'Another thing I want is a man who is useful, who can cope with emergencies about the house. Matt should be hands-on with his house, painting and plastering, instead of being here playing with his computers.'

Tessa felt an even stronger temptation to tell her what she had learnt about Matt, but she was bound by her promise.

'Anything else?' she asked.

'That's enough to be going on with for me.'

'If you won't settle for anything less than the ideal man you're likely to end up on your own.'

'Maybe that is safer than choosing the wrong man.' Diane sat up and forced a smile. 'Come the end of our holiday, I'll say goodbye to Matt and I'll have forgotten him by the time our plane touches down in England. Now let's forget about men. What are we going to do tomorrow?'

'Wander into town early on, shop for souvenirs, have coffee, back here for lunch and siesta, then a glass of wine by the pool before dinner. That's what I plan to do, but you and Matt may have other ideas.'

'He's already said he's busy tomorrow morning, so I'll come shopping with you. Incidentally, there were some new arrivals today and one or two of them looked quite promising.'

'I'm off men and you're already suited for the duration of the holiday,' Tessa reminded her.

'There's no harm in having a spare!'

The next morning was a very agreeable outing. Shops in the narrow streets were combed for suitable souvenirs. Tessa was beginning to wonder whether she would be able to fit it all in her luggage. The only interruption was when Diane suddenly pulled Tessa into a doorway.

'Quiet!' she hissed. 'That awful Valdes man is coming this way. I don't think he saw us and with any luck he'll just walk past us.'

They waited for several seconds, but there was no sign of Valdes. Tessa risked putting her head out of the doorway to see if he was still visible. He was, but he certainly had no attention to spare for English tourists. He was backed against a wall, trapped there by two hulking men, and seemed to be having a violent argument with them.

'Come on! Let's slip away while he's dealing with those two,' she murmured, and rapidly the two girls quietly hurried to the next turning.

'It looked as if he might be in real trouble,' Diane said, looking back.

'Then he deserves it. He probably played some nasty trick on them, and I hope they make him pay for it,' Tessa said firmly.

Afterwards they took a long break for

coffee and people-watching in a sunlit café by the sea before wandering slowly back for lunch. As they left the restaurant and entered the foyer Tessa saw Rose Hunt at the reception desk. She waved to Tessa.

'How did the shopping go?'

'Very well — plenty of souvenirs for the family and friends.'

Rose smiled, then glanced at Diane and lowered her voice.

'Could I have a word with you?'

'Certainly. Diane, I'll see you in five minutes.'

The two went into the lounge, which was almost deserted at this time of day.

'It's only a small thing,' Rose Hunt began. 'You know the ring your friend was given?'

Tessa nodded.

'The one with the blue stone which Matt gave her.'

'That's the one. Well, in the old days I used to have some quite good jewellery and while your friend seems to think it's just a piece of costume jewellery, it looks the real thing to me.'

'You think it's real gold?'

'I think it's real gold and a real sapphire. Of course I didn't have a chance to examine it properly, and I may be wrong, but she should definitely take good care of it.'

'Thank you for telling me what you think,' Tessa said slowly. Rose couldn't realise what problems this information caused. Diane might panic if she thought Matt was giving her valuable gifts and decide he was getting too serious, and there was also the question of whether Matt could afford such a generous present for a brief acquaintance if his house was eating up all his money. Diane certainly didn't want a boyfriend who was reckless with money. That would remind her of her parents. How profitable were his computing activities? As she went to join Diane in her room she decided not to tell Diane what Rose thought about the ring. After all, as she had said, she might have made a mistake.

7

When the two girls came out of lunch, Rose Hunt was near the entrance to the restaurant, chatting animatedly with a tall man whose back was towards them. Rose caught sight of them and waved, and her companion turned to see what had attracted her attention. He was lean and dark-haired, with a wide, humorous mouth, and looked about thirty-five. He smiled at the newcomers as Rose led him over to meet them.

'Just the people we need!' she said brightly. 'Tessa, Diane, meet John Slade. He arrived this morning and was asking me about the area round here, and I had to confess that I'm shockingly ignorant about it because I've scarcely set foot outside the hotel. I know Tessa has been busy exploring since you came here, so I am sure you can give him more information.'

'I'm a sightseer rather than a sunbather,' explained John Slade. 'I know there are some famous caves near here, but there must be more to see.'

'Come and have coffee with us and I'll try and tell you what I've found out,' Tessa offered.

'I'd like to do that.'

His smile was warm, showing white teeth.

Rose Hunt turned away.

'Aren't you coming for coffee as well, Rose?'

Rose shook her head.

'I've something to do so I'll leave John with the two of you.'

'Thank you for your help,' John Slade said hurriedly. Tessa saw his eyes follow Rose as she walked away, and saw Rose pause and look back at him before she went outdoors.

In the lounge Tessa, with some contributions from Diane when it came to shops, tried to give John Slade some idea of what he could see in the area.

'It sounds very promising,' he commented. 'I look forward to exploring the neighbourhood.'

'Of course Tessa could show you herself,' Diane interjected.

Tessa glared at her, but John Slade's slow smile seemed to show genuine pleasure at the suggestion.

'I should like that very much — unless you have other things to occupy you?'

'Nothing at the moment,' Tessa had to admit, still looking daggers at Diane.

'Well, I am planning to catch up on some sleep this afternoon, but perhaps we can meet for dinner and then we can plan an outing or so.'

He left soon afterwards, trying to stifle his yawns, and Diane looked after him smugly.

'You didn't have to tell him I had nothing else to do, Diane! The poor man had no option then but to behave as if he wanted to come out with me.'

'I think it was a good idea. He's an attractive man who likes looking at things, so you might have found someone who suits you and you can spend your time with him for the rest of your holiday.'

'Leaving you free to spend all your time with Matt when he's available without worrying about me!'

'True, that is another advantage, but I think you might enjoy yourself as well. You must admit he's better than that awful Gordon, or that horrible Valdes. Valdes has come back safely, by the way. He must have persuaded those two thugs to let him go unharmed. I saw him chatting up the young receptionist.'

'I suppose John Slade does look reasonably healthy,' Tessa said thought-fully, shuddering at the memory of Gordon.

John Slade was waiting near the restaurant door when Tessa went down for dinner with Matt and Diane. They had just settled at a table for six when Rose Hunt appeared. She saw them and came over too. She nodded greetings to all of them, and then addressed John Slade.

'Was I right? Was Tessa able to help?' she enquired.

'Indeed she was,' John Slade told her, and then stood up and drew out an empty chair. 'Are you on your own? Why don't you join us?'

Rose hesitated, looking at the others, obviously reluctant to intrude on the foursome.

'Please do!' Tessa urged her, remembering their previous talks and grateful for her help.

Rose smiled and then slipped elegantly into the seat.

'In that case I will. I spent lunch listening to all the symptoms of my neighbours' various ailments, and I don't want to spend another meal like that.'

It was an enjoyable, animated dinner. Rose's conversation was lively, amusing and sometimes bordered on the slanderous when she was discussing other guests, and her younger companions soon forgot the age difference between themselves and Rose. But afterwards she refused to join them for coffee, excusing herself on the grounds that she would have to return to her usual companions before her desertion hurt their feelings.

'But we'll meet again?' John Slade enquired.

She smiled into his eyes and put a hand on his arm.

'I'm sure we will.'

While Matt and Diane murmured to each other, Tessa and John Slade discussed where they could go in the next few days. He and Tessa seemed to have similar tastes and she was delighted to think that with him as a companion she would be able to explore places that Diane would not have wanted to visit.

She met him at the foyer the next morning, as they had agreed. Once again he was talking to Rose, who greeted Tessa with a smile.

'I understand the two of you are off

to explore Spain. Enjoy yourselves. I prefer the poolside.'

In fact Tessa enjoyed the morning very much. The sun shone warmly on the two of them as they sauntered through the narrow town streets, and he proved a perfect companion, interested in what she could show him and with an eye for detail which added to her own knowledge. Apparently he had an interest in architecture and his comments on the influence of the Moors on Spanish architecture led to a discussion on the long history of the Moors in Spain, and what they had left behind. Over coffee they exchanged some more personal information. He sympathised with her over her job loss and wished her well when she went back to England. He was a solicitor and was, as she had thought, in his late thirties, and lived in Cheltenham.

'I'm on my own now,' he told her. 'I did have a long-term partner, but we wanted different things from life and gradually we drifted apart. We stayed friends — in fact she invited me to her wedding a few months ago. I wasn't sure of the etiquette, so in the end I sent a present but I didn't go.'

Tessa decided he would make an ideal elder brother, but that there was no chemistry, no likelihood of any romantic feelings developing between them. A pity. Her mother would definitely have approved of him. She found herself mentally comparing him with Tom Collins, but they were so different that she was unable to decide which one of them was to be preferred. John was her intellectual companion, but she could not forget those moments in Tom's arms. John would never arouse the same passion in her.

Occasionally she thought of what Diane had said about her attitude to Tom. It was true that none of her former boyfriends had had a profession that involved manual labour. That was just chance, she told herself uneasily. She then tried to imagine herself telling her mother about Tom and could visualise the unspoken disapproval which would be shown in a slight twist of the mouth, the advice to look for someone 'more our type'. Her mother would definitely have preferred John Slade.

Even while she was enjoying John Slade's company, from time to time she found her thoughts drifting to the farm among the avocado orchards and the people she had met there. It was only natural curiosity, she told herself. Of course she wanted to know what was happening to Joaquin and his children and whether Tom had regained his solitude. At one point she realised that John had stopped talking and was looking at her with a slight frown.

'Is anything the matter? You seem to be miles away.'

'I'm sorry,' she said hurriedly. 'I was just wondering whether I'd got enough presents for my family.'

His smile was a little patronising.

'Women always seem to be thinking about shopping.'

It seemed to be taken for granted that Rose Hunt would join them for dinner that night. Tessa noticed the way John made her very welcome and spent much of the meal talking to her, though Rose once again did not stay with them after the meal.

'I'm surprised a woman like that is on her own,' John commented as he watched her walk away.

'There are reasons,' Tessa said, and told him about the death of Rose's husband.

He nodded understandingly.

'She'll find someone else,' he said confidently. 'It's just a matter of time.'

The next day Matt emerged late in the morning from yet another prolonged session of work, eager to please Diane and make up for his absence.

'Let's skip dinner at the hotel tonight,' he suggested to the other three over lunch. 'Why don't we all go into town and have dinner at some restaurant? It will be a change to have waiters looking after us instead of queuing up at the buffet. Somebody was telling me that they'd been to a restaurant there that serves very good Spanish food.'

'It would make a change,' Diane agreed. 'Are you happy to do that, Tessa?'

'Certainly. A change would be fun, and I'd like to try some real Spanish food. John?'

'Count me in.'

Tessa and Diane decided it was the right occasion for their best dresses, with only light jackets needed to protect them from the cool evening air. Tessa thought that the occasion merited wearing her silver and amethyst necklace and opened the room safe to take it out. While the safe was open she took the opportunity to check how much money she had left. She counted the notes, counted them again, and then sat back, frowning.

'What's the matter?' Diane enquired. 'If you're running short of money I can let you have some.'

'I was sure I had eighty euros left,'

Tessa said slowly. 'But there are only forty here. Two twenty-euro notes seem to have gone missing.'

'Are you sure you had eighty? Perhaps you spent more than you thought when we went shopping the other day.'

'I counted what I had left after we got back. At least, I think I did.'

'Don't worry. The money will probably turn up in your handbag or in a jacket pocket. No one can have taken it from the safe.'

Tessa nodded, though reluctant to believe she could have been so careless.

'I expect you're right. Forty should be enough for the next couple of days anyway.'

John Slade noticed her necklace and admired it as they prepared to stroll towards town along the road that ran parallel to the sea.

'I like good jewellery,' Matt commented, with a sideways glance at the ring on Diane's hand. He saw Tessa looking at him and grinned sheepishly.

They stood on the hotel steps and looked up at the star-filled sky.

'Just think what it's like in England now,' Tessa said. 'According to the weather forecast there's plenty of rain and cold winds.'

'We'll be back there in a few days,' Diane reminded her and pretended to shiver.

'And I'll soon follow you,' John added.

'Not me. I'll still be here basking in the sunshine,' boasted Matt.

'When you're not stuck in your room with your computer,' Diane said sharply.

'How much longer do you expect to be here, Matt?' Tessa enquired.

He shrugged.

'I had an email saying that work on my house is going well, but I'll probably be here for another four or five weeks, possibly longer.'

'Don't you want to get home, back to your own house?' John Slade enquired.

'I suppose so. But I live by myself, and it can get a bit lonely, and I'm not terribly good at cooking.'

Conversation died away as they walked along. Matt and Diane were holding hands, content to be in contact with each other with no need for words. Tessa could hear the quiet roar as the surf broke on the beach and the constant stir of the thousands of fruit trees the fertile soil supported. She breathed deeply and smelt the perfume of the flowers that grew in gardens or blossomed in the fields. England and the search for work was a long way away. She found that at some point John had taken her hand. She let it stay in his light grasp, then looked across at Diane and saw the expression on her friend's face as she murmured something to Matt. She was convinced that Diane would find it a lot harder to say goodbye to Matt than she thought. She wondered whether she and John would reach the point of exchanging addresses before she went home. It would be nice to have him as a friend, though nothing more.

The restaurant was not difficult to find. It was on the outskirts of the town, looking towards the distant hills, so that in the summer diners would be able to sit on the large terrace at the front and enjoy their meal and the spectacular views at the same time, but now, in February, the terrace was empty but the interior of the restaurant looked warm and welcoming as Matt held the door open for the two girls to enter.

'Tessa! Welcome!'

It was Manuel advancing to greet her, arms spread wide in greeting, a beaming smile on his face. She laughed with surprise and allowed herself to be kissed on both cheeks.

'You have left your hotel for my restaurant?' he said in mock surprise.

She decided it would be tactful to hide the fact that she had not known that this was the place he owned.

'So many people at the hotel recommended you that we had to come.'

At least that was partly true!

'And you will enjoy your meal,' he promised, ushering the four to a table with a scrubbed wooden top and linen napkins. 'Do you know anything about Spanish food?' They shook their heads. 'Then let me choose for you.'

Without waiting for an answer he swept away to the kitchen, clapping his hands for attention and issuing orders to the unseen cook. The others looked at Tessa enquiringly.

'Another acquaintance you've made?' Diane asked.

'He's the man I told you about, the one who gave me a lift back the other evening. I didn't know this was his restaurant, however.'

'He's obviously delighted and flattered that you've come here, so we won't tell him that.'

Manuel returned with a bottle of red wine and filled their glasses with due ceremony. Soon afterwards he was back again, accompanying the waitress who was carrying dishes of food to their table. She was a comfortably plump girl, plain but with a beaming smile, and Manuel introduced her as his daughter, Sofia.

'She will look after you well,' he promised.

A short time later they looked up when there was a disturbance at the door. Someone was trying to come in but Manuel was blocking their way, refusing admittance, and a man's voice was raised in protest. At one point Manuel was almost thrust aside, and Tessa saw that the would-be diner was Pedro Valdes. She groaned. He seemed to be everywhere she went, spoiling things. But not this time. A waiter appeared to help Manuel and together they shut out Valdes. Manuel came to the table to apologise for the disturbance.

'The man was drunk,' he told them, 'and I will not have drunks in my restaurant.' He hesitated. 'I think he was drunk. His eyes looked strange — he might have been on drugs. Anyway, he is not coming in here, so please forget him.'

They settled down to enjoy themselves. They were brought a selection of small dishes containing various savouries, tapas, and these started the meal, whetting their appetite. The main course was a braised game bird, slowly cooked till it was meltingly tender and enriched with a red wine sauce thickened with herbs and vegetables. They thought they were too full for dessert until Manuel served them with a dish of fresh fruit and a deliciously rich ice cream which had very little in common with the commercial varieties. To accompany it Manuel also produced a carafe of sweet white wine.

'You will like it. It is made by a cousin of mine.'

Coffee came with brandy and he waved away their protests.

'You are walking back to your hotel and it is getting late. The brandy will keep you warm.'

It was while they were relaxing over their coffee and brandy, enjoying the memory of the meal and not yet ready to make the effort to start on the walk back to the hotel, that they heard a voice greeting them.

'Good evening.'

They looked up to see Tom Collins, dressed in his old jeans and an open-necked shirt.

His sudden appearance left Tessa without words at first, surprised by the sudden rush of pleasure she felt at the sight of him, and then she remembered to introduce him to John Slade, who nodded and gave a brief smile. Matt and Diane had already met him briefly at the hotel door, of course.

'I just dropped in for coffee and a word with Manuel. Do you mind if I join you?' Tom asked.

'Of course not,' Tessa said as the others indicated their agreement. She shouldn't be so surprised to see him, she told herself. Hadn't he said he often ate at Manuel's?

Manuel was already pulling a chair out for his friend. Tom sat down and there was a moment's awkward silence, broken by Diane.

'Hallo, Tom. I've only seen you briefly, but Tessa has been telling me all about the children and their father, and how kind you were to them.'

Tessa was full of questions she was longing to ask.

'If you're here by yourself, does that mean that they have left the farm? Where are they now?'

Tom pointed at the ceiling.

'Above us.' He laughed at their puzzled faces. 'Manuel had a crisis. A woman who works here part-time had to leave suddenly to go to Seville to look after her father, who's had a stroke. Manuel thought of the meal Joaquin cooked for us, contacted him through me, and offered him her job while she is away. They still needed somewhere to live, but there are a couple of rooms above the restaurant which have been used for storage but are empty now, so the family have moved in there and Joaquin is working for Manuel. There's a school for the children nearby, so it's all turned out well for them.'

'But will he get enough for the three of them to live on?'

'He's also going to be working for me from time to time when I need help, so he'll just about be able to get by. It's not an ideal solution and I don't know how long the arrangement will last, but their problems are sorted for the time being.'

Tessa nodded. She could imagine Joaquin's relief.

'So you're a jack-of-all trades?' John commented. Was there a patronising note in his voice?

'That's how some people would describe me,' Tom said curtly, and then turned his attention to Matt.

'So you're the computer man?'

Matt laughed.

'That's how people would describe me. Are you interested in computers?'

'I know a bit about them, though I only have a fairly basic laptop. What

213

exactly do you do?'

The conversation between the two men became technical while the others sat quietly finishing their coffee and brandy. Tessa stopped listening and contented herself with observing the two men deep in discussion. They were very different. Matt was tall and dark, a happy extrovert, but she decided that although Tom was less striking at first glance, quieter and more self-contained, he was equally attractive in his way. She caught Diane giving her a knowing grin and hid a smile.

'If you ever need a web-site set up, let me know,' Matt was saying. He fished a small white card out of his pocket. 'Here are my contact details.'

'Thank you, but I doubt if I'll need one soon. So far I haven't got further than an advertisement in the local paper and this,' and Tom pulled out his own card.

'I wish I had your practical skills,' Matt said ruefully. 'I suppose Tessa told you that I'm here while my house is being repaired. I've had to leave it to the professionals because I'm hopeless with my hands.'

John Slade, who had sat silent while the other two men talked, looked at his watch ostentatiously and Matt sighed.

'I suppose it's time to get back to the hotel,' he said. 'Why don't you call in there sometime and I'll show you what I do properly? I'll be here for another few weeks by the look of things.'

'Thank you,' Tom responded. 'I might do that.' He turned to Tessa and Diane as the little group stood up, ready to leave. 'I hope you've enjoyed your meal. Perhaps we could all meet here another night?' His gaze passed over John Slade, apparently accidentally omitting him from the invitation.

'We have enjoyed the meal, but I don't think we'll have a chance to repeat it. Diane and I only have three more days before we go home,' Tessa reminded him.

She was pleased to see how his face

fell. So his own company wasn't always enough!

'Which means this is probably the last time we shall see each other,' he said heavily.

'I suppose so.'

They looked at each other. Tessa suddenly felt that there was a lot they should have said to each other, but that it was too late now.

'Once again, thank you for your help. I couldn't have coped with the children without you, and every time I see them they keep asking when they are going to see you again,' he said awkwardly.

'I enjoyed it, on the whole, and give my love to the children,' and she held out her hand. 'Goodbye.'

He took her hand in both of his and she felt again the work-hardened warmth of his grasp.

'Goodbye.'

Then suddenly he lifted her hand to his lips and kissed it before releasing her and turning away, striding off and out of the door without another word.

John Slade watched as he walked away.

'Another ex-pat scraping a living,' he commented.

Tessa was suddenly angry.

'He happens to be doing very well,' she said coldly.

'Really? Well I think he should invest a bit more money in his clothes.'

'We'd better go as well,' Matt said hastily, looking at his watch. 'I'll just settle the bill. This evening's on me.'

John Slade made a token protest, but when Matt called for the bill, Manuel scoffed and waved aside any suggestion that they should pay for their dinner.

'It is my way of saying thank you to Tessa for helping my friend Tom. If she hadn't done that I would not have Joaquin working for me now. I will not take your money.'

As they left, Tessa saw the two business cards still lying on the table. Neat as ever, she scooped them up and into her handbag.

They strolled back to the hotel,

pleasantly sleepy by the time they reached it. Tessa said a brief goodnight to John and left Diane to take her own leave of Matt. She saw a notice had been put up by the reception desk about their flights back to England and spent a few moments reading it. It brought home to her how soon she would be leaving Spain. Afterwards, on her way to the lifts, Tessa glanced into the lounge and saw that John Slade had evidently decided that it was not yet time for bed. He was standing in a quiet corner talking to a woman whom Tessa was not surprised to see was Rose Hunt. While she watched, Rose lifted a hand to John Slade's face. It could have been a friendly gesture, but it seemed to last a fraction too long for that. Interesting.

When Diane joined Tessa in their room she said how much she had enjoyed the evening.

'And now I've met him properly I like your Tom.'

'He's not my Tom!' Tessa said

emphatically. 'I was glad to hear that Joaquin and the children are settled for the time being, but otherwise I think it was an unfortunate coincidence that Tom showed up tonight.'

'Coincidence?' echoed Diane. 'Don't be dim, Tessa! Matt and I are positive that after we appeared at the restaurant Manuel was on the phone to Tom at the first opportunity, telling him you were there.'

Tessa sat up in her bed, appalled.

'Do you really think so?'

'We do. And the really interesting thing is that as soon as he heard the news, Tom came hurrying to the restaurant so quickly that he didn't even wait to change his clothes in case he missed you. He wanted to see you again. And he was not at all pleased to find you were there with John Slade!'

Tessa groaned and sank down, pulling the covers over her ears.

'Take me home, back to England! Life is getting too complicated here!'

Tessa and John Slade had agreed to

visit the famous caves near the little town the next day. After his cool reaction to Tom, she now regretted that arrangement but she could not think of an acceptable excuse and therefore met him the following morning as arranged.

They caught the local bus into town and then had to find one which would take them on to the caves. As they walked along, John suddenly stopped and caught Tessa by the hand.

'What's the matter? You've hardly said a word since we left the hotel.'

'Nothing's the matter,' she said defensively.

'That's not true, Tessa. It's obvious that I've done something to upset you.' He paused. 'Is it because of what I said about your friend Tom last night?'

Tessa was silent, but John shook his head in self-reproach.

'I'm sorry. I know I sounded an awful snob. I didn't mean to.'

'You sounded just like my mother,' Tessa said fiercely, and then stared as he burst into laughter.

'Is she really so bad?'

Reluctantly at first, Tessa found herself joining in his laughter.

'I am really sorry,' he said penitently at last. 'I'm afraid I've definitely been conditioned by my middle-class upbringing. I think our mothers must be very alike. And I have to admit I was a bit annoyed when he appeared without warning and spent most of the time gazing at the girl I was supposed to be with.'

'Don't pretend you were jealous!'

'Not jealous, but my masculine pride was hurt.'

'You're talking nonsense!'

He sighed.

'Look, I apologise for my behaviour. Now, can we forget last night and enjoy this morning?'

After that Tessa was able to relax a little and enjoy the dramatic cave system, but there was something else on her mind, a subject which she finally broached when they had emerged from the caves and were having coffee.

'John,' she said, putting her cup down, 'I want to talk to you about something, and I don't want you to get upset.'

He looked at her warily.

'That sounds serious.'

Tessa drew a deep breath.

'Why are you here with me?'

He looked at her in bewilderment and she went on.

'We get on quite well and I think you've enjoyed my company these last few days, and I've enjoyed yours, but I'm pretty sure I am not your first choice. You would much rather have been here with Rose Hunt.'

His cup crashed into its saucer.

'Good heavens, Tessa, what made you think that? Mrs Hunt is a very pleasant woman, but she's years older than I am.'

His voice faded away under Tessa's steady stare.

'I've seen the way you look at her,' she said. 'Your voice changes when you talk to her. It's lower, more intimate.'

He picked up his cup, took a gulp of coffee, fiddled with the handle and refused to meet her eyes. Then he sat up, put the cup down again, and looked straight at Tessa.

'You're right, of course. I like you, just as I like Diane. But when I look at Rose I get a very different feeling. I feel close to her, as if we'd known each other for years, and she excites me. But she's too old for me.'

'And is the age difference the only reason you are here with me instead of with her?'

'Isn't it enough?'

'Why? You're years older than I am but that doesn't seem to trouble you.'

'That's different. People would talk about a man and an older woman,' he said wretchedly.

'And does that matter more than being with her? Aren't you being a coward?'

He looked at her indignantly, then sighed and shook his head.

'Suppose she feels the same way

about the age gap? Suppose I tell her how she makes me feel and then she rejects me, laughs at me?'

'Suppose she doesn't? Think of that and take a chance.'

The silence stretched out, and then he nodded slowly.

'You're right. It's my upbringing again, of course. But Rose is more important than a little gossip, or the risk of a little hurt pride.'

Tessa stood up.

'Then why are we still sitting here? Don't waste any more time. Let's get back to the hotel.'

He stood up as well, then suddenly leant forward and kissed her full on the lips.

'Thank you, Tessa.' Then he burst out laughing. 'At least you've made it perfectly clear that you're not interested in me. Is it the plumber?'

'No!' she snapped. 'I just hate to see you wasting your time.'

As they neared the hotel John's stride grew longer. He was walking faster and faster, as if he couldn't wait to see Rose again.

When they reached the hotel they saw Rose dozing on a sun bed by the pool. John Slade took a step in her direction and then hesitated. Tessa gave him a sharp push in the back.

'Go on!' she hissed.

He approached Rose and sat on the sun bed beside her. As she turned lazily to greet him he leant forward and said something. She opened her eyes, frowned, and shook her head. He said something else and she sat up and stared at him. Then she smiled slowly. Watching, Tessa smiled as well and then went indoors.

At the reception desk an elderly woman was complaining loudly to the manager.

'It must have been one of the staff who took it!'

The manager shook his head firmly.

'I can assure you the staff are perfectly trustworthy, and none of them had any reason to go near your room at that time.'

'But someone did go into my room! They must have had a key.'

Tessa looked enquiringly at a woman who was standing by, clearly listening to every word.

'What's happened?'

'She left her purse in a drawer by her bed,' the woman murmured, 'and she says that when she went back to get it quite a few euro notes had been taken from it.'

Tessa went up to her room, making a mental note to make sure her few valuables were always locked away in the room safe. Diane was in the room already, resting and reading a book. She greeted Tessa and looked at her suspiciously.

'What have you been up to? Why are you looking so smug?'

'I've just brought two people together. They should enjoy the rest of their holiday.'

She told Diane about John and Rose while her friend listened, wide-eyed.

'She is very attractive of course — for

226

her age. But you do realise that this leaves you on your own yet again?'

'Don't worry. After Gordon and Pedro Valdes, I'll enjoy a couple of days by myself.'

She hoped her friend had not noticed that she had not included Tom Collins in the list of men she didn't want to see again.

8

That evening John Slade and Rose Hunt came into dinner together and sat at a table for two, clearly oblivious of everybody else. Matt had had the situation explained to him, and the girls had been amused by the way he had been obviously rather taken aback.

'I suppose it's all right here, on holiday, away from the people they know, but it might be a bit awkward back in England,' he said dubiously.

'Times are changing, Matt,' Diane teased him. 'In a few more years I might be looking round for a younger man.'

'Not if I can help it!'

'But you won't be there,' she reminded him.

He fell silent, and Tessa saw how they both seemed to lose their animation and avoided looking at one another.

Things improved towards the end of the meal, however, when they heard a polite cough, looked up, and saw the head waiter standing by their table, beaming and holding a bottle of champagne.

'Are we celebrating something?' Tessa asked. 'Is it your birthday, Matt?'

Matt shook his head and the waiter hurried to explain.

'This is for you with the compliments of the gentleman over there,' he told them, indicating John Slade, who smiled and waved. Tessa smiled happily back as Rose blew her a kiss.

There were two full days of holiday left, and Tessa planned to do some more shopping, go for walks on the beach, and finally take plenty of photographs to show her parents, but in spite of these good resolutions the next day found her walking along the dirt roads through the fruit trees towards Tom Collins' house. She had spent some sleepless hours during the night thinking about this. She was aware that in spite of what Diane had said he did not seem particularly eager to see her, but she had enjoyed his company and, anyway, she wanted to find out a little more about the fortunes of the children and their father. Finally she had decided that she would follow the path to his house, sure that at least she would not get lost again. If she got there and the house was empty, then at least she would have had a pleasant walk and some good exercise. If he was there then they could meet as friends who had been through a lot together in a surprisingly short time. Reading the hotel notices, she had found something which gave her another excuse.

She set off, telling herself that she would find the place deserted, with Tom working away somewhere, but as she rounded the last bend her heart began to beat faster as she saw him busy at a low wall, scraping out old mortar. She approached quietly so he did not hear her coming and she stood watching him, noting the efficiency and economy of movement, the easy grace of his body, and felt once again the physical response within her body which he alone had aroused in her.

Then something seemed to alert him to her presence and he swung around and then stood upright, easing his back.

'This is a surprise! Have you come to help mix some concrete or is something the matter?'

She shook her head and held up her camera.

'Everything is fine, I just felt like a walk through the trees, taking photographs before I go back to the hotel.'

He rubbed his hands on his jeans, leaving dusty streaks.

'You're just in time for a morning coffee.'

Once again he brought mugs of coffee out to the table, no longer needing to ask how she took it. They exchanged a few casual remarks about the weather, how much they had enjoyed Manuel's restaurant, then Tessa decided to deliver the message that had really brought her here.

'Tomorrow night is our last night, and there's a dance at the hotel. I wondered whether you'd like to come and join our party.'

He did not respond immediately.

'Thank you for the invitation,' he said at last, 'but I'm usually too tired after a day's work to go socialising in the evening.'

Her heart sank. She would have enjoyed his company — as a friend — but now she would spend the evening with Matt and Diane, feeling completely superfluous. She forced a smile.

'Oh well, it was just an idea.'

His eyes were straying back to the wall and the abandoned tools beside it. He was obviously eager to resume work.

She stood up.

'Goodbye, then. I'll be on my way.'

She took one last, long look at the house.

'I can understand why you care so

much about this. It's a house to be loved.'

He nodded slowly, his eyes fixed on the white walls.

'It's meant to be a family house. I had dreams of living here with Lucia and our children. The other night, when it rained and the children were upstairs in the big bed and you were beside me, it seemed for a while as if my dreams had come true.'

She looked at him.

'And when you kissed me, were you kissing me or Lucia?'

He stood still, and then gave a helpless shrug.

'I don't know.'

She turned and left him.

Back at the hotel she did not tell Diane about her visit to Tom. After all, he wouldn't come to the dance, so there was no need for her to know how humiliated Tessa felt by his refusal.

When the last full day came and she started doing some preliminary packing, Tessa's feelings were mixed. Her stay here had been more eventful than she had expected, but it had all been very different from her life in England. Now it was time to return to that life — to real life.

'By this time tomorrow we will be back in England,' Diane said dolefully as they seized their last opportunity to sit by the pool. 'It will be grey and cold, and it will probably be raining and the next day we'll have to start job-hunting.'

'I've been thinking about that,' Tessa said lazily, half-asleep on her sun bed. 'I don't want to make the same mistake again and end up in another dead-end job just because it's safe. I think I'm going to sign on at an agency that supplies secretaries to firms when they are needed temporarily. That will give me a chance to experience a range of businesses, and when I find one I like I can try and get a permanent job there.'

Diane perked up.

'That sounds a good idea. I might try it as well.'

'So long as they don't send us back to Mr Briggs!'

They both spent a lot of time getting ready for the dance that was to be held that night. Rose Hunt had warned them that this fortnightly event was an excuse for all the female hotel residents to display their best finery. Diane wanted to look her best because it would be her last evening with Matt. Even though she hadn't got a partner, Tessa was equally determined to look as good as she could. She took out her silver and amethyst necklace, then decided reluctantly that it wouldn't go with the dress she had chosen and she put it back in the safe.

Matt met the two girls in Reception and after paying both of them elaborate compliments he escorted them into the lounge, where tables and chairs had been moved to the sides to leave more room for dancing. Rose and John were already there, and Rose was obviously upset about something, frowning and twisting her hands together while John tried to comfort her.

'What's the matter?' Tessa asked anxiously.

'I've been robbed!' Rose said bitterly. 'My gold brooch has gone! It is quite valuable, and it was also an anniversary present from my husband.'

'Where did you leave it?' Tessa asked, remembering the other woman who had claimed to have had money stolen from her purse, and her own missing euro notes.

'I left it in the safe in my room, but I didn't know it was gone till I looked for it tonight because I wanted to wear it,' Rose said miserably. John seemed about to speak but she waved him to silence impatiently. 'I know! You think the same as everybody else — that I must have left it somewhere in my room, or worn it and lost it, but I know I put it in the safe!'

All Tessa could do was offer her sympathy and then go to join her friends, leaving John to distract and comfort Rose.

Tessa had feared that she would spend most of the evening sitting alone while Matt and Diane danced together, but this was not the case. Matt, obviously instructed by Diane, danced with her a couple of times, and there were several elderly but spry gentlemen who welcomed the opportunity to ask a pretty girl to dance. At the end of one particularly energetic quickstep she was returning gratefully to her table when she was joined by Matt and Diane, who were also coming back from the dance floor. Suddenly Tessa stopped, her hand going to her throat. Tom was standing by their table.

'Hello, Tessa,' he said quietly, his attention focussed on her alone. Then he hastily remembered his manners and greeted the other two who, instead of sitting down as they had intended, walked away with over-obvious tact, saying they were going to the bar. Tessa was left facing Tom. He looked serious, even a little grim, his hands in the pockets of a suit which was perfectly presentable, even if it was a little tight across the shoulders.

'I didn't think you'd be coming tonight,' she told him, almost accusingly. 'You didn't sound very keen when I told you about it.'

'To tell the truth, I didn't know myself if I would come this evening till about an hour ago. I didn't know whether you'd be pleased to see me or not. I thought you might be too occupied with your new boy friend and just find me a nuisance.'

So Diane had been right. When she had referred to 'our party' he had thought she would be with John Slade and had been jealous. She laughed.

'If you mean John Slade, he's not my boy friend, and if you look over there, you'll see him dancing with the woman he really cares about.' As he stared at Rose and John, holding each other closely as they danced, she said tartly, 'Now, are we just going to stand here, or can we sit down?'

They sat down on opposite sides of

the table, which seemed to symbolise the gulf between them, and there was another silence.

'So why did you come?' Tessa demanded suddenly.

'I wanted to see you once more, even if it's only to say goodbye yet again.'

Suddenly Tessa felt that she was full of happiness.

'I'm glad you did.'

Now, finally, he smiled at her.

'In that case,' he told her, 'let's dance.'

Helped by the music and the wine, it was a magical evening. Though the two couples shared a table, each pair was almost unaware of anybody else. Held closely in Tom's arms, Tessa was vividly aware of his masculine strength as he guided her round the floor. She felt the roughness and strength of his hands on her bare arms. She noted the way his hair grew at his temples, and wanted to touch it and then follow the shape of his clean-cut mouth with her fingers. It almost seemed he could read her thoughts, for he smiled at her and held her even closer.

'Why did you think I might not want to see you? Was it just John?' she asked at one point.

'After what was said yesterday, I was sure you wouldn't want to see me.'

'But you still came.'

'As I said, this was my chance to see you for the very last time.'

They were silent for the rest of the dance, aware that her approaching departure the next day inevitably cast a shadow on the evening's happiness.

It was nearing midnight when he led her outside, saying that they needed some fresh air.

* * *

In the moonlit garden he took her hands in his.

'Tessa, I did a lot of thinking after you left me yesterday. I loved Lucia very much, but she has been dead for two years, and I still have a life to live.'

Then, standing under the palm trees, with the faint sound of the surf in the background and the starlit sky overhead, he kissed her, gently at first and then more urgently. She responded eagerly, once more feeling her body respond to his. At last he lifted his head, released her and stood back, still grasping her hands.

'Come to the farm with me,' he said hoarsely. 'We can have one night together. Come with me now.'

She thought of the white-washed farm with the avocado trees whispering round it, and of the great double bed waiting for them, and her first impulse was to agree, to go with him and share with him her last night in Spain. But one cold, clear part of her mind had not yet been swept away by her desire.

'One night together?' she queried. 'No commitment, no obligation?'

'No commitment, no obligation,' he repeated.

Suddenly her hands were pushing him away.

'That's not for me,' she said. He stood there, trying to follow her change of mood. 'Please, go now,' she said tiredly. 'I've got a long day tomorrow and I need some rest.'

He still stood there and her voice rose.

'Go away!'

'Tessa . . . ,' he began, but before he could say more they heard Diane's voice. She and Matt had just come out and had seen them.

'Hello, you two! It's getting a bit hot inside, isn't it?'

Tom muttered something which might have been agreement but could have been a curse.

'I need a nice, cool drink,' Matt said firmly. 'If you'll come with me, Tom, we'll get a bottle and some glasses.'

'It's about time I went,' Tom said brusquely. 'I've got a lot to do tomorrow.'

'You can stay for a farewell drink,' Matt urged him.

'Well, maybe I could do with a drink.'

The two men went off together and Diane moved closer to Tessa.

'I'm sorry, did we interrupt something?'

'Nothing special,' Tessa lied.

The men returned, Matt with a tray of glasses, Tom grasping a bottle, and the drinks were poured.

'Here's to a great holiday,' Matt said, holding his glass aloft.

The others echoed him, Tom and Tessa avoiding each other's eyes.

The wine finished, Matt turned to Diane.

'Another dance?'

When they had gone, Tom turned to Tessa.

'I'm sorry that I messed up our last evening together,' he said painfully. 'I'll never forget you or the way you've helped me.'

Tessa mumbled something incoherently, then sat down on a low wall and looked up at the hotel, avoiding his gaze.

Suddenly she tensed and stood up,

craning her neck.

'What's the matter?' Tom demanded.

Tessa hesitated.

'Our room's just there,' she said pointing. 'Just above that palm tree.' Her voice trailed off and she went on staring upwards, frowning. 'I know I turned the light off when we came out, but there is a light in there now.'

'You might have left a bedside lamp on.' Tom peered upwards and Tessa heard him take a sharp breath. 'That's not a room light. It's moving about. It's somebody with a torch!'

Tessa gave an undignified squeak.

'It might be a thief! Somebody has been stealing from rooms.'

She stood up.

'I'm going up to see what's going on.'

'Wait! If it's a thief it might be dangerous. We'll tell the manager.'

'And if we wait he might have gone, taking our things with him!'

She ran indoors towards the lifts, Tom close behind her.

'Get the manager!' she snapped at

the girl on the reception desk. 'There's an intruder in our room.' Tom stopped momentarily to give the receptionist more details, calling to Tessa to wait, but Tessa ran on. She knew that what she was doing was rash and could prove dangerous, but the physical action helped distance her from the mental turmoil of the recent scene with Tom. She reached the lift, pressed the floor button, and the doors closed in Tom's face. When it reached Tessa's floor she hurried towards the door of her room and gave it a gentle push but it did not move.

'It's still locked,' she said to herself shakily. 'Maybe I made a mistake.'

She fumbled in her evening bag for the key card, inserted it, turned the room handle, and threw the door wide open. The room, lit only by the lights outside, was empty. Tessa took one step inside, then two, feeling extremely foolish. Then suddenly she was seized from behind and a hand was clamped across her mouth.

'Keep quiet, you stupid, stupid woman! Why didn't you stay at the dance with your plumber boyfriend?'

She recognised the voice. It was Pedro Valdes.

'Now I shall have to tie you up so you can't raise the alarm before I get away.' He gave an ugly laugh. 'Maybe I can spare a few minutes to amuse myself with you, to revenge myself for the way you and your friend have treated me.'

She was shivering with fear, and he laughed again.

But just then there was the sound of someone running along the corridor, fast, and Tom burst into the room.

'Tessa! Where are you?'

He saw her, held prisoner by Valdes, and stopped.

'The manager is coming with the security men,' he said grimly. 'Let her go.'

Valdes suddenly released Tessa, pushed her aside, and snatched up a large torch which he had obviously abandoned on the bed, and as Tom approached him

246

Valdes gripped it like a club and swung it at Tom's head. Tom dodged, knocking a chair over, but the torch still hit him a glancing blow hard enough to hurt, and Tom gasped with pain and then, furiously angry, hit Valdes in the stomach with the full force of his body behind the punch, and as the man folded over Tom took him by the front of his shirt and shook him like a dog. Valdes twisted and struggled, but just as it looked as if he would break free there was the sound of more footsteps in the corridor and the manager and two security men arrived. After that, there were no problems. Valdes saw that escape was impossible and stood sullenly still.

Tessa saw that the wardrobe was open, and the safe door, and then she gave a wail and pounced on her silver and amethyst necklace which was lying on the floor where Valdes had dropped it.

Meanwhile the security men were roughly searching Valdes, extracting from his pockets various small items of jewellery and handfuls of bank notes.

'Are you all right, Miss Saunders?' the manager asked anxiously. She nodded, rubbing her neck where Valdes had held her.

'We will send for the police,' the manager told Tom and Tessa. 'Now I will telephone Senor Valdes as well and tell him that his son is a thief!'

This threat galvanised Valdes into frantic protests.

'No! The police, yes, but don't call my father!'

The manager ignored his pleas and, held fast by the security men, Valdes was taken down to the ground floor. As he was forced through the door he snarled at Tom.

'I slashed your tyres but that was not enough! I should have slashed you and burned down your little house as well!'

Tessa locked her necklace away again in the safe. Nothing else seemed to have been touched. Their passports and tickets were safe, useless to a thief.

She stood up and pushed her hair

back from her face and laughed shakily.

'Well, I didn't expect that to happen. And it's not long past midnight!' The laugh faded. 'My legs feel wobbly.'

Tom, still breathing heavily, put his arm round her to support her and she turned to him and buried her face in his chest for an instant, then lifted it and stood back.

'It's time you went.'

He looked at her for a long moment, and then nodded.

'I hope everything goes well for you,' Tessa managed.

He gave a small smile.

'Have a happy life, Tessa.'

He leant forward and kissed her gently on the cheek, then turned and left the room. Soon she heard the lift door closing and the murmur as it began its descent.

She sank down on the bed and a few tears crept down her cheeks. She wanted so much to say yes, to go with him to the little farm. But she had been aware, deep down, that one night would not be enough for her. She wanted love as well as passion, a companion for life. Thank heavens she would be flying away from Spain tomorrow. Then she looked up, surprised, as the door opened and Diane came in, slamming the door shut angrily. Tessa sat up, hurriedly wiping her face with her hand.

'What's the matter? I thought you and Matt . . . '

Diane sat down heavily.

'There is no me and Matt.'

Then she saw the traces left by the recent disturbance in the room, things still lying on the floor and the chair tipped over.

'What's been happening?'

'Tom was rescuing me from a burglar,' Tessa told her.

Matt was temporarily forgotten as Diane demanded more information, but Tessa was still puzzled.

'I didn't expect you back here tonight. What went wrong?'

Diane sniffed and fumbled for a tissue.

'I thought we understood each other, that I'd made it very clear that this was a holiday romance and that after tonight it would be over. Then Matt started talking about love, and refused to accept that we would not see each other again. He assumed I hadn't really meant what I said about a holiday romance, and that as soon as he told me he loved me I would fall into his arms and promise to stay with him for ever. He told me that he's got a big house and has made quite a lot of money from computing. Then he asked me to marry him and said that the ring he bought me was real gold and sapphire and he saw it as a kind of engagement ring. So I threw it at him and told him to get lost and came back here.'

She burst into noisy tears and Tessa scrambled to put her arms round her friend and hug her. Finally the sobs stopped and Diane sniffed noisily.

'What happened to you before you saw the light in the room?' she asked at last. 'We couldn't see either of you when we finished dancing, so Matt and I thought you were together somewhere.'

'Tom wanted to have me for the night and then say goodbye forever,' Tessa said wryly, painfully aware that Diane had rejected what she wanted so badly. 'I think we should have switched boy friends.'

Diane was laughing and crying at the same time.

'Oh, well, let's get our party dresses off and go to bed. Tomorrow morning we'll leave both of them behind us.'

Tessa still held her friend.

'Diane, are you sure you are doing the right thing? Maybe you are making a big mistake about Matt.'

Diane sat up, pushing her away.

'I've told you that I don't want love, a long-term commitment,' she said fiercely. 'My parents claimed they loved each other once. I'm not going to risk making the same mistakes.'

Tessa sighed.

'If you are sure . . . '

Diane nodded firmly.

'Don't mention him again.'

'Well, in that case let's forget about boyfriends. After all, what we do when we get home is more important.'

When they went down for an early breakfast the following morning, the manager was waiting to speak to Tessa. He took her into his office.

'I wanted to see you before you left, to tell you about Valdes. I'm sure you will understand that we want to keep the story of Senor Valdes's thefts as quiet as possible,' he said anxiously, and smiled with relief when she assured him that she would not gossip about it.

'Valdes' father had sent him here on behalf of the firm, but it was not an important job. Really he was just an errand boy. However, he decided that his father was not allowing him enough money for his expensive tastes. Somehow he managed to get master keys to the hotel rooms and the master code for the safes. He has been flirting with one of the reception girls, and I am afraid she may have been careless with security when he was around. Anyway, he began helping himself to small amounts of money, small enough so that people were not sure whether they had mislaid it rather than having it stolen. Then he learnt that his father was coming, and he knew he would not be able to explain where he had got enough money to enable him to live as he has been doing, to hire that showy sports car he's been driving, for example, so last night he was taking all the valuables and money he could find while people were at the dance, intending to run away with the proceeds. Fortunately he had not taken much before you saw the light in your room. The jewellery has been recovered and returned to its owners and the hotel will reimburse people who have lost money. So, on the whole, everything will be cleared up satisfactorily and quickly.'

'I'm glad,' Tessa said sincerely. 'I like

this hotel and I like the staff, and I am glad they have been cleared of any involvement except for one silly girl.' She hesitated. 'I'm supposed to be flying home today. Will the police want to speak to me?'

The manager shook his head.

'Mr Collins is witness enough to what happened in your room, and other guests who were robbed won't be leaving for some time.'

That was a relief!

Matt did not appear for breakfast while Tessa and Diane ate a hasty meal before they finished packing. There was no sign of him an hour later when they took a last look at the view from their room, went downstairs, and said good-bye to various guests they had got to know. The coach arrived to take them to the airport and as they left the hotel Tessa took a quick look at the car park but Tom's little white van was not waiting there.

As she went to climb on to the coach she heard her name being called. She turned eagerly, but it was Rose Hunt who was running out of the hotel.

'I slept late after the dance and I thought I'd missed you,' she panted, seizing Tessa's hand. 'I just wanted to thank you for helping John realise how he felt about me. I haven't had a chance before.'

Tessa hugged her.

'I didn't do much. I just had to give him a little push. He'd have acted without me eventually.'

'Possibly, but it would have meant that we would have had even less time together.' Her smile was sad. 'I know that for various reasons we probably won't stay together once we leave here, but at least we will have the rest of the holiday to remember, and I am very grateful.'

The driver was fidgeting, anxious to depart, and Tessa and Rose gave each other a quick kiss and then the older woman stepped back from the coach, and she was the solitary figure waving as they drove away.

At the airport they checked in, and at the door to the Departures Lounge they both gave one last look behind them, but neither Tom nor Matt came dashing into the airport building to beg them to stay. Their plane was on time, they boarded it, and it took off.

They were silent for the first hour, each deep in thought. Then Tessa looked at Diane.

'Well, it was an interesting fortnight. Are you sorry we went?'

Diane hesitated, then shook her head emphatically.

'No! There were some good times, things I'll remember for the rest of my life.'

Tessa thought of Maria and Juan playing in front of the farmhouse, the warm glow of the lamps lighting up the room at night, the scent of the trees carried on the wind. She remembered the touch of Tom's hands, the warmth of his body.

'You're right. Let's remember the good things and forget the rest.'

9

Mr Saunders was waiting at the airport and greeted them warmly.

'Well, you seem to have survived,' he commented, regarding them both critically. 'It was a good holiday, then? Better weather than we've had here?'

'Very good weather and a good holiday,' his daughter replied firmly.

He dropped Diane off at her flat and then drove Tessa home. Her mother flung the front door open as the car drew up on the drive and rushed out to greet her daughter as though she had been away for two years rather than two weeks. Once she had hugged her and kissed her she held her at arm's length and examined Tessa carefully.

'You've definitely caught the sun. Are you sure you put enough sun cream on?'

'Quite sure, Mother. Now can we go

indoors? I've really missed your tea.'

This produced the desired result as her mother hurried to put the kettle on while her husband brought Tessa's case indoors. She found the souvenirs she had chosen so carefully and presented them to her parents, who accepted them with cries of delight, and then the cup of tea was followed by the expected questions on the hotel and its food, and what she had seen of Spain. Once these queries had been answered, her mother was eager to pass on the latest gossip and neighbourhood news. Tessa listened and tried to appear interested, but felt as if mentally she was still halfway between Spain and England, not really connected to either. She pleaded tiredness and went to bed early. She woke in the night and felt surprisingly lonely, missing the gentle sounds Diane made when she slept.

She was woken in the morning by the sound of rain on the window, and went downstairs to find her mother complaining that the milkman had left full-fat milk instead of semi-skimmed. Suddenly Spain seemed a long way off in distance and time. This was real life.

That afternoon she went shopping to replace some of the toiletries she had taken on holiday. When she returned she saw a car parked outside her home, and recognised it as Eric Lester's. She had almost forgotten about him and went in slowly, almost reluctantly, to find Eric in the living room having tea with her mother. He stood up when she went in but his greeting was limited to 'Hello, Tessa,' and a smile. He did not approach her or say anything about missing her or enquire about her holiday.

'Look who's called in, Tessa,' her mother exclaimed. 'I'll just get another cup for you,' and she disappeared.

Tessa sank down.

'Did she call you to say I was back?' she asked bluntly.

'There was no need. I phoned when you didn't appear at the restaurant as I expected and she told me you'd gone to

Spain and so I asked when you'd be back.' His gaze was mildly reproachful. 'I was very surprised to hear it from her. Why didn't you tell me you were going away?'

'It was all booked at very short notice,' she found herself explaining defensively.

'There was so much to do that I'm afraid I forgot about our date.'

'I understand.' He smiled forgivingly. 'And was it worth rushing off in such a hurry?'

'Yes! I had a wonderful time.'

'I'm glad to hear it. You must tell me all about it tomorrow.'

'Tomorrow?'

'I thought perhaps we could go out for the dinner we missed, if that's all right with you.'

Why not? It would be falling into the old routine she had tried to escape but she wasn't doing anything else and it was easier to say yes than no, easier to go out with him than make excuses and then try to explain to her mother why the prospect of dinner with Eric did not thrill her.

'I've got nothing planned,' she told him.

At that moment her mother obviously decided that she could no longer delay returning with the extra cup, and after a little general conversation Eric left.

'I'll see you tomorrow, Tessa,' were his parting words, and Tessa saw her mother's satisfied smile.

Tessa had no great hopes for the evening out but in fact she enjoyed her dinner with Eric more than she had expected. It was pleasant to be greeted warmly and by name by the Chinese girl, and Eric seemed to be making an effort to please her and listened to her heavily edited account of her Spanish holiday attentively and spent less time than usual talking about the rather boring aspects of his job at the bank.

'I did miss you when you were away,' he assured her, and at the end of the meal, when he saw her fumbling in her handbag, he shook his head.

'No. I insist on paying for both of us. It's my way of saying welcome home.'

'Are you sure?'

'Quite sure. Now, about our next meeting, if you're not planning to go to India or Japan . . . '

She found herself agreeing to meet him the following week without hesitation.

When they were leaving he helped her on with her coat. His hand rested on her arm for a second. It felt smooth and soft, unlike Tom's work-worn hands. But that was another world.

The next week it was obvious from his wide smile and general smugness that he was very pleased about something. He would not explain what it was, but said that he might have some very good news to tell her the next time they met. His good humour persisted through the meal, though this time he did not offer to pay her share. A couple of days later he telephoned to say that he had booked a table for them at one of the best restaurants in town for the following evening.

'I'm celebrating!' he announced.

Tessa decided that the Michelin-starred restaurant deserved a new dress and raided her dwindling savings. It was grey and lilac on a white background. She looked in the mirror and fingered her silver and amethyst necklace which went with it perfectly, remembering how she had almost lost it to Valdez. Her mother admired the dress when Tessa appeared in it and was even more delighted when she learnt why it had been bought and where Eric was taking her daughter.

'Their chef was on television the other week. It must be a very special occasion if he's taking you there. Has he hinted at anything?' Her eyes lit up. 'Do you think he missed you so much while you were away that he realised he's in love with you? Perhaps he's going to propose!'

'No, I don't think so. The celebration is something to do with his work,' Tessa said firmly, and saw her mother's face fall.

The restaurant was quietly luxurious. Tessa was impressed, and Eric obviously enjoyed her reaction, though he gulped visibly when he saw the prices. However, he steeled himself and even ordered a bottle of house wine.

'What are we celebrating?' Tessa wanted to know.

He smiled complacently.

'We are celebrating my promotion to senior assistant manager at a larger branch of the bank. In a few years I can expect to be managing my own branch.'

This was indeed a big step up. He seemed to accept Tessa's warm congratulations as his due.

'It's not just the status, though that is significant, of course. I will also get quite a big rise in salary, enough to be able to afford a decent house, one big enough for a family. I can start planning the future.'

He was looking at her significantly, and suddenly she realised what he was implying and why she was being treated at such an expensive restaurant. Her mother had been right. He did intend to propose. Tessa was to be part of Eric's plan for the future, part of his family, established in his new house. Did he mean to propose that night? She felt panic rising. She needed time to think what her answer would be.

'I see you like amethysts,' he remarked, looking at her neckline. 'Perhaps one day you will have a ring to match that necklace.'

It was not a proposal but it was another very strong hint that once he had bought the house and decided on his personal aims, his next purchase would be an engagement ring for Tessa.

Fortunately it appeared that he was not yet quite ready to make his intentions explicit and propose formally. He explained carefully that he would have to spend some time settling into his new post before he could start planning his private life.

'The branch is about fifty miles away

so I won't be able to come back to see you each week. I'll miss you, but perhaps that problem can be solved. The bank is in a very nice area. I'm sure you'd like it. When I start house-hunting you must come and help me choose.'

She could imagine the neat detached house he would want, with a garage for his cherished car and a fitted kitchen. Unbidden, she had a sudden memory of Tom's white farm house with its primitive washing and cooking facilities.

Tessa lay awake that night, wondering what she would say when Eric finally made his intentions clear and asked her to marry him. There was no denying that many women would accept him without hesitation. He offered comfort and security, and would make a reliable and efficient husband and father. What more could Tessa hope for? Suddenly she sat up in bed. If she married Eric Lester it would be a practical move. She did not love him, but he would give her comfort and security, and she would be the house-keeper he needed and give him children. But at intervals throughout the evening she had found herself comparing Eric Lester with Tom Collins, and now, suddenly, without any warning, she realised why. She wanted to go back to the white farmhouse, the orchards of fruit trees speckled with blossom and murmuring in the wind. She wanted to go back to Tom Collins! She loved him! She had told herself again and again that she was thinking of him so often simply because of the physical reaction he had stirred in her, and had laughed at herself for letting her body distract her mind. But now she realised how she ached to be back in the warm white room, his arms round her as they sat in the light of the oil lamps. She wanted to feel his kisses once again, to give herself to him completely and wake up next to him in the great bed. But the bodily longing wasn't all. It didn't matter that she had only known him a short time. It had been long enough to see his kindness, his capability, to learn his dreams for the future. It had been long enough to make her love him. But she had realised that too late and would never see him again. And he might want her, but he did not love her. At least, now she knew she could never settle for Eric. She lay down again, tears creeping down her cheeks.

She was not the only one having problems. Tessa and Diane had carried out their plan and joined a secretarial agency. Most days there was work for them, though Tessa found that moving from firm to firm was stimulating but tiring. No sooner had she found her way to one firm, learnt what they wanted from her and gained a smattering of the internal politics, than she was moved somewhere else and had to start all over again. A couple of firms did offer her permanent work, but neither appealed to her. Diane was having the same experience, but Tessa did not think her friend's low spirits were entirely due to work.

'What's really the matter, Diane?' she challenged her when they met to compare their current employers. She had noticed the dark shadows under her friend's eyes, the sad droop of her mouth when she thought Tessa was not looking.

Diane avoided her eye, crumbling her cake nervously.

'Life seems so dull at the moment. There's nothing to look forward to.'

'Well that's the same as before we went away.' When Diane did not reply Tessa leant forward. 'It's Matt, isn't it?'

Diane pushed her chair back as if about to stand up and walk out, but then, slowly, very slowly, she nodded. There were tears in her eyes when she looked at Tessa.

'I thought I'd get over him, that I'd soon forget him, but I can't. He was special.' She sighed. 'I've told you that my parents' marriage was such a disaster that it's put me off marrying anyone in case I take after my parents and everything goes wrong, as it did for them. And the more I felt for Matt, the more scared I was as I struggled against my feelings, and the more I told him that I didn't really care for him or want to see him again.'

'Couldn't you contact him so that you can tell him you've changed your mind?'

'After what I said to him that last evening he'd never take me back, no man would.' She managed a smile. 'If I've made a mistake it's too late to do anything about it. He's probably back in England now, working away at his computers and glad I did refuse him. Now, how about your love life? Any more news about the banker?'

Tessa explained about the situation with Eric, but did not feel ready to disclose her full feelings about his impending proposal or about Tom. How could she, when she was still coming to terms with them herself?

'He might propose at any time, and I suppose I've given him good reason to expect me to say yes, so I honestly don't know what I'm to do about him.'

Diane frowned.

'You know, Tessa, from what people say about men, your Eric seems to be ideal husband material. But I don't know. You don't want to spend the rest of your life being bored silly. And, frankly, you don't even seem to like him very much.'

Tessa sat back and nodded her agreement with her friend. Her decision was confirmed.

'You're right! I can stand him for a few hours — for a meal or a visit to a cinema — but I couldn't spend days, years, with him. He is extremely boring, and I don't feel any affection at all for him.'

'Then you can't marry him. It's that simple. Now, let's change the subject. I've heard some news about our old boss, Mr Briggs. Soon after we left the owners of the firm realised how hopeless he was and fired him.'

'No! Who told you that?'

'Miss Carter. I met her in a shop yesterday and she told me all about it.'

'She must be devastated. How can she survive now?'

Diane giggled.

'We don't have to worry about her. The owners installed a new, efficient manager. Apparently he's quite young and Miss Carter is having a great time mothering him and he seems to like it.'

'Good! I'm glad she's had some good luck at last.'

Later, at home, Tessa brooded on Diane's situation, comparing her uncertainty about Matt to her own relationship with Tom. Several times Tom had made it clear that he did not want commitment, that Lucia had been the only woman he had wanted to share his life. At least, she congratulated herself, she had told him almost as often that she wanted freedom as well, together with the creature comforts that urban living provided. Suddenly she froze, staring blindly at the wall. Had he believed she really meant it? Had they both been protesting too much, alienating the other? She twisted her hands together, thinking back over what they had both said. Well, as Diane had said about her situation, it was too late to do anything now. Wasn't it?

The next day she called Diane.

'Meet me at our usual coffee shop at six o'clock tonight,' she instructed her. 'Don't be late. This is really important.'

When Diane arrived Tessa was already there, sitting bolt upright and looking very serious.

'What is it?' Diane said, shrugging her coat off. 'A crisis at work? Or has Eric proposed?'

Tessa took a sheet of white paper out of her handbag.

'This is an email I've printed out. It's confirmation that I have booked two return tickets to Malaga. Southern Spain, in two days' time, on Friday morning.'

Diane stared at her friend.

'You're going back to Malaga? Why, and why two tickets?'

'One is for you and one for me. We're both going back to Malaga, Diane.' Diane was about to explode into speech, but Tessa held up her hand. 'Wait. That's not all I've done. I found Matt and Tom's business cards in my handbag and I have emailed both of them, telling them that we are coming back to Spain and when we will be landing at the airport.'

Diane was scarlet, almost exploding with rage.

'I'm not going to beg Matt to take me back! It would be too humiliating if he turned me down!'

'So you're going to let pride stop you ever seeing Matt again, even though you've realised how much you care about him?'

'He might not even be there any more!'

'Tough luck — but if he isn't he can email me to say where he is. You've got to find out, Diane.'

Something occurred to Diane and she looked at Tessa almost accusingly.

'You're not just doing this for me because you like match-making and you want to hand me back to Matt. What about you? Why have you emailed Tom Collins? I thought you weren't interested in him.'

Tessa held up her hands in a gesture of surrender.

'It's confession time. I've changed my mind. It took me some while to realise how much I do care for Tom, time to contrast him with Eric Lester, time to contrast my life here with what it would be in Spain. Now I know what I want, and it's Tom.' She took a deep breath. 'Look, Diane, it's up to them now. If they don't want to see us then they won't meet the plane. There won't be any face-to-face confrontations. But we must find out how they feel.'

Diane was shaking her head in disbelief.

'Tessa, you're supposed to be the sensible one, and now you've come up with this hare-brained scheme where we are chasing a man who probably left

Spain weeks ago, and another who's shown no sign of wanting you for more than a quick night together. You've gone mad!'

'Probably, but I'm going to be on that plane to Malaga, and I hope you will be as well.'

'And if they don't appear, what do we do then?'

Tessa shrugged.

'Find a hotel, visit some museums, have a few meals out and catch the flight back on Sunday evening, go to work as usual on Monday.' She gazed at her friend. 'Come on, Diane, let's take a chance. We wouldn't have met them if you hadn't insisted on going to Spain, so now let me be the one who takes us back.'

Diane sank back in her chair and finally, very slowly, nodded.

'All right, but what are you going to do about your banker?'

'I have plans,' Tessa said mysteriously. She grinned. 'I'm going to have a bit of fun with Mr Lester.'

10

Once Diane had agreed to the reckless adventure, she threw herself wholeheartedly into making plans. It showed how much she really cared about Matt, thought Tessa, how much she wanted to discover if he was still in Spain, still longing for her. She herself was not prepared to settle for Eric now she had finally realised how much she cared for Tom, but Eric was obviously sure that she was waiting for him to propose to her and eager to accept him. Now, rather than simply rejecting him, which could lead to accusations that she had misled him, she had to persuade him that she was not the girl for him after all.

They met the next evening at the Chinese restaurant. Tessa had spent some time plotting her tactics. First of all she shook her head when asked if she wanted the usual order and instead asked for the most expensive dishes on the menu. Eric raised an eyebrow, but he said nothing. After all, he expected her to be paying her full share. Instead of agreeing to a glass of house wine with their meal, this time she pointed at an expensive bottle of white wine on the list.

'Let's have that one, Eric.'

He looked at the price and closed his eyes momentarily.

'I don't think so, Tessa. It's not really my type.'

'Oh, come on. I'd like it and you can afford it!'

She spoke loudly enough for near-by diners to hear and Eric realised that they were listening, curious to learn what he decided. He looked wretchedly at the girl impassively waiting for their order. Forced to choose between money and pride, Eric felt compelled to choose pride, and reluctantly ordered the wine. He was quiet for a few minutes afterwards, but by the main course he had apparently decided to overlook the matter and had begun to talk of houses near his new posting.

'I can't decide yet between a semi-detached and a detached house. A detached house would be an investment, but I don't want to spend too much straight away.'

'If I were going to move there,' Tessa said with a meaningful look, 'I would insist on a detached house with at least four bedrooms. After all, a senior assistant bank manager has to live up to his status. You'll have to buy a bigger car as well, Eric. I know you claim your present one is very reliable but it's not impressive enough.'

Eric managed a laugh.

'I'll be an assistant bank manager, Tessa, not the actual manager.'

She pouted.

'You said you would get a big increase in salary.'

'I will be getting more, but I won't be rolling in money.'

'Oh.' She held out her empty glass.

'Pour me some more wine, Eric.'

He obeyed, frowning. When he stopped pouring she continued to hold her glass out till he topped it up.

'You seem to be drinking more than usual, Tessa,' he commented.

'Yes, I seem to have got the taste for it in Spain, particularly for good wines.'

He was almost silent for the rest of the meal. At the end, when the bill was brought, he carried out his usual careful calculations and told Tessa how much they would each have to pay. She fumbled in her bag and frowned.

'I must have left my purse out when I changed bags. I haven't any money.'

'What about your credit card?'

'I haven't got that either.' She smiled at him. 'I'm afraid you'll have to pay the lot, Eric.'

The bill, including Tessa's expensive dishes and the wine, came to almost double the usual amount, and Eric paid with a very bad grace and Tessa saw that the girl who served them was trying hard not to laugh. Eric did not say a word in the car and when he dropped her at her parents' house he did not give her the usual peck on the cheek, nor did he mention seeing her the following week. She watched him drive off with a sense of relief as well as a trace of guilt. He would now be considering whether Tessa's new expensive tastes and liking for alcohol disqualified her as an assistant bank manager's wife and she could guess what his verdict would be. If her venture to Spain failed, she would have to find another companion for dinner at the Chinese restaurant.

Then she had to tell her parents that she was going back to Spain for a few days at very short notice. She told them that someone she and Diane had met on holiday had invited them back for a special party. Her news was not well received.

'You can't go all the way to Spain just for a party!' her mother wailed.

'It costs less than taking the train to London,' Tessa pointed out. 'We're going on a cut-price airline.'

Her father sat watching his daughter, saying very little until her mother had gone out of the room.

'Do you want me to take you to the airport?' he asked her then.

She nodded gratefully.

'Then tell me why you are really going.'

'For a party . . . '

'Nonsense.'

She stared at him defiantly.

'I want to go back because I've realised that I am in love with someone I met there, and I have to find out if he loves me.'

She clenched her fists as she waited for her father to tell her how stupid she was being, to tell her to think of Eric, but instead her father's eyes were dancing.

'That is very romantic!' he exclaimed.

Tessa gaped at him.

'I thought you'd disapprove.'

'I should, of course, but I'm not going to! I've always hoped you'd do something romantic.'

'But I was sure you and Mother wanted me to marry Eric Lester.'

'Well, your mother thought he would suit you. You've always been so practical, so sensible . . . '

'You mean so dull?'

Her father fidgeted.

'Let's just say that I agreed that the two of you seemed to suit each other, but now I am delighted that you are going back to Spain.'

'The man I love is a plumber and electrician when he isn't being a farmer,' she warned him.

'So what? Your great-grandfather was a bricklayer. I've heard that plumbers are in great demand in Spain. He could go on to build a business empire.' He had the grace to blush. 'All right, perhaps I am getting carried away a little. At least we would be able to spend time with you in Spain. I've always fancied a holiday there.'

Tessa gave up.

On Friday morning Diane was

waiting to be picked up.

'Are you going to support Tessa in her search for romance?' Mr Saunders asked as he picked up her bag. Diane looked at Tessa and giggled.

'What have you told him, Tessa?'

'Diane has her own reasons for wanting to get back to Spain, Father,' Tessa murmured.

He laughed.

'Both of you? Is Spain ready for this? I can't wait to hear what happens!'

They arrived at the airport in good time. Diane thanked Mr Saunders and started towards the airport doors while Mr Saunders took his daughter in his arms.

'Do you think you'll be coming back on Sunday?' he asked her.

She smiled, tears starting to her eyes.

'Probably. And if I don't, it will be for a very good reason.'

'In that case, don't worry about your mother. Once she realises how romantic it all is she will be thrilled.'

Then it was the usual routine of

checking in. Both of them had brought only hand luggage, half-expecting their stay to be very brief. Then they sat patiently through the hours in the plane, staring out of the window at the clouds below them in the stormy sky. When the plane landed they took their bags from the overhead lockers and without speaking they walked through Customs and into the Arrivals area, both tense and wondering if anyone would be waiting for them or if they had made complete fools of themselves.

There was a cluster of people waiting to welcome the arrivals from England and Tessa looked at them eagerly, but then her heart sank. There was no one waiting for them, no one that she recognised. Oh, well, there were several places to go sight-seeing in Malaga and they were only there for the weekend. She gave Diane a twisted grin and shrugged. She just hoped that her friend would eventually get over her disappointment and forgive her for dragging her to Spain on a wild-goose chase. But Diane was not looking at her. Instead she made a strange choking noise and Tessa saw that she was staring incredulously at a tall man with short dark cropped hair, dressed in a smart business suit and carrying a briefcase. It was only when he smiled at Diane and she saw his dark eyes that Tessa realised that this elegant businessman was Matt. Diane stood in front of this unexpected vision, shaking with laughter, until Matt dropped his briefcase, took her in his arms, and silenced her with a kiss. Tessa sighed, suddenly feeling very alone. She would be visiting the museums by herself.

Eventually Matt's embrace slackened. With his arms still holding her, Diane turned to her friend, her eyes shining, but then her face fell as she saw Tessa's expression and she gently moved away from Matt and put an arm round Tessa's shoulder.

'I'm so sorry! Tom Collins is a fool!' Tessa tried to smile.

'Oh, well, it was a gamble and at least

it has worked for one of us.'

Now Matt had picked up both their bags.

'I'm still based at the same hotel, so I've booked the two of you a room there. Shall we get a taxi?'

'Please, Matt.'

They moved toward the exit, with Diane holding Matt's arm as if to make sure that he was really there, and he smiled fondly down at her.

'Incidentally,' he remarked in the taxi, 'I've also booked us in for dinner at Manuel's tonight.'

'We'll enjoy that,' Diane said enthusiastically. 'Won't we, Tessa?'

'I suppose so,' Tessa said grumpily.

'Good. And I emailed Tom Collins and asked him to come as well, though I haven't had a reply.'

This information was greeted with silence. Matt looked at Diane in surprise, and Tessa saw her quickly shake her head and put her finger to her lips.

The hotel was unchanged, though a

veil of green in the gardens showed that spring was nearly there. The holiday-makers were of the same elderly age-group, though with unfamiliar faces.

They had had sandwiches on the plane so didn't feel the need for lunch. Instead they went straight up to their room, which was very near the one they had had before, with the same view, but Tessa hardly noticed. She threw her shoulder bag on the bed furiously, her deep disappointment turned into anger.

'Why didn't he come to the airport? After what we went through together, he could at least have come to say hello! Why should he avoid me? I'll never forgive him!'

'I don't know, Tessa! Wait and see if he does come to dinner.'

'I'm not coming to Manuel's. I'm not going to sit there feeling a fool while you and Matt drool over each other.'

'You must come! When Matt hears how we came to come back he will want to thank you. And suppose Tom does come and you aren't there?' She looked at Tessa hopefully. 'Meanwhile, would you mind if I left you on your own for a bit? Matt wants to go for a stroll along the beach with me. We've got a lot to talk about.'

Tessa plumped down on the bed.

'Go on, don't mind me. I'll unpack.'

Her friend still hovered anxiously and Tessa forced a smile.

'Go to Matt! At least, my scheme has worked for you and Matt, so make the most of it.'

'I'm entitled to sulk,' she told herself when Diane had gone. 'I arranged that we come back, I bought the tickets and sent the emails, and it's Diane who's all happy and starry-eyed.'

She tried to feel pleased for her friend's sake, but it was difficult, especially when Diane returned from her walk glowing with happiness and eager to tell Tessa what had happened.

'We talked,' she said. 'I told him why I am against commitment, why I believe that romantic love rarely lasts. Like you, he said that often love does last, even if the first excitement wears off. Then, Tessa, he asked me again to marry him! I told him how ridiculous that was when I'd just been saying why I couldn't commit myself to a long-term relationship. He said he understood that, but that he was sure that he wants to be with me for the rest of his life. He said I didn't have to say yes or no to his proposal now, but that if I do change my mind and decide I want to be with him, I just have to tell him and we'll start planning the wedding!' She held out her hand. 'Look!'

The sapphire and gold ring shone on her finger.

'It sounds as if it is all going well for the two of you,' Tessa commented, trying to muster some enthusiasm, but Diane looked at her and frowned, momentarily forgetting her own happiness.

'I suppose you haven't heard from Tom?' she ventured. 'No telephone calls?

I did think he might have been working this afternoon and just couldn't get to the airport.'

Tessa shook her head.

'He obviously isn't interested in me.' She stood up. 'Let's forget him. We're going to have a good time without Mr Collins!'

At that moment the telephone rang. The two girls looked at each other, and then Tessa picked up the receiver.

'Tessa Saunders here.' Diane saw her hand grip the receiver but Tessa shook her head at her friend. 'Yes, I remember, of course.' She listened for a couple of minutes. 'That's very interesting. Thank you for letting me know.' She put the receiver down and turned to Diane. 'That was the manager. You remember that awful young man, Pedro Valdes?'

'The one who thought he was God's gift to women, and then you and Tom caught him stealing your necklace? What about him?'

'Well, the manager noticed we were

back and thought I might like to know what happened to him. The hotel rang Pedro's father after he had been arrested and told him what his son had been doing. His father was here within a couple of hours, absolutely furious, of course, and from what the manager said I think Pedro Valdes would have preferred to be handed over to the police straightaway! Anyway, all the jewellery was recovered and his father repaid the money that had been taken, so the hotel and its guests were happy.'

'Good!'

'Good for the hotel, and I gather they think Pedro Valdes will get what he deserves when he comes to trial.'

The next morning it was taken for granted that Matt and Diane would go off together while Tessa stayed at the hotel. The growing warmth made sitting by the pool with a book seem a very good idea, and Tessa was just getting settled when she heard her name called.

'Tessa! What are you doing back

here? I thought I'd never see you again.'

It was Rose Hunt and Tessa sat up to welcome her.

'Don't bother about me! I thought you were going back to England ages ago!'

Rose sat down.

'I did. But we've come back — just for a week.'

'So have Diane and I. Coincidences do happen.' She did a double take. 'We? Do you mean you and John Slade are here together?'

'Yes — and before you try to be discreet, we are sharing a room.'

'Congratulations!'

Rose's smile was a little wistful.

'I'm not sure that congratulations are in order. We've come back so we can discuss the future on neutral ground.'

Tessa looked at her closely. There was a difference about Rose, not so much in her appearance as in her manner. There was more animation, more life, but obviously something was worrying her.

'Can you tell me the problem? After

all, I am the one responsible for the two of you getting together.'

Rose stretched out her long, shapely legs, and looked at her toes.

'John wants us to move in together,' she said flatly.

Tessa stared at her.

'But that's marvellous! But you don't think so. Why not? Have you got so used to living by yourself that you don't want to give up your freedom . . . ?' Her voice trailed away. She was thinking of Tom Collins.

Rose was shaking her head.

'No! I would love to think we could spend the rest of our life with each other.'

'What's the matter then?'

'We spent two very happy weeks together here. Then we went back to England. We had discovered we don't live a long way apart, so John came to see me a couple of times. He stayed with me and we met my friends as a pair.' A slight frown appeared. 'Some of them were determined to be up-to-date and tried to behave as if the fact that my boyfriend was so many years younger than I am didn't surprise them. A couple took me aside and pointed out that when I was seventy John would be in his fifties, and that might cause trouble. I had thought of that, but I thought it would be worth it if we could have a few good years together.' She fidgeted. 'Then I went to stay with John and he took me to see his sister and her children. She and her husband were marvellous. They just accepted me.'

She fell silent. Tessa waited and finally Ruth heaved a sigh.

'The trouble is that I saw how he enjoyed family life and playing with his nieces and nephews.' She bowed her head as if to hide tears. 'I can't give him children, Tessa, though he says he doesn't mind, that he enjoys seeing his sister's children but he doesn't want any of his own. But I think he will regret not having them eventually, and might come to hate me for it.'

Tessa knew that she could say nothing to help and eventually Ruth sat up and pushed her hair back.

'I don't know what we'll decide. We love each other — now. There's no question about that. Should we give that up because of possible future problems? Should I accept that our relationship probably has no future? Or should I stop worrying about the future and be happy with John while I can?' She turned to Tessa. 'What ever happens, I shall be grateful for the happiness I have found. John has given me my life back. After my husband died I was just existing, passing time without any real purpose. Now I've woken up. I am going to decide what to do with the rest of my life, and I'm going to find a purpose.'

Tessa held out her hands to the other woman and they hugged each other.

'Whatever you decide, Ruth, I wish you well and I wish you happiness.'

'Thank you. And you?'

'I came here with Diane and now she

and Matt are reunited I shall enjoy the sunshine by myself.'

'No romance for you? What about that man you were with at the dance? You looked very close.'

'I thought we were, but unfortunately I've found that romance seems to avoid me.'

'It can come very unexpectedly. Look at me.'

Then John Slade appeared and greeted Tessa with surprise and pleasure before the two of them went off together. Tessa watched them go and wished them well.

Showering and changing for dinner that evening brought back memories of the last time Tessa and Diane had gone to Manuel's restaurant. Tessa wondered what had happened to Joaquin and the children. At least Manuel should be able to tell her that, and with a little discreet questioning she should be able to find out what Tom had been doing in her absence. With a sinking heart, she realised that she was taking it for granted that Tom would not be there that evening.

There was a smell of fresh green vegetation as they walked along the sea front. The trees in Tom's orchards would be covered with blossom. Diners were not yet sitting on the restaurant's veranda, but the windows had been opened to allow the scents of the early spring air to drift in.

Manuel greeted them with kisses, with an extra one for Diane.

'My friend Matt will be happier now you are back,' he told her.

Apparently Matt had got into the habit of dining there from time to time and had become friendly enough with the proprietor to tell him how much he was missing Diane.

'What happened to Maria and Juan and their father?' Tessa enquired when Manuel was pouring the first glass of wine.

'Joaquin?' Manuel's face split in a broad grin. 'Sofia should tell you about him.' As she went to ask what he meant, he held up a finger. 'Wait! I hear someone coming.' He span round. 'My friend Tom!'

Tessa almost dropped her wine glass. It was indeed Tom, dressed in fresh jeans and shirt, with his hair still damp from the shower. He greeted them without a smile, looking a little tense.

'Hello, Tessa, Diane. Thanks for inviting me, Matt. I'm sorry I'm a bit late. A lady called in a panic because a pipe had burst in her bathroom and water was dripping through her kitchen ceiling.'

'I'm surprised to see you at all. You weren't at the airport,' Tessa said coldly.

'I was! But I probably got there minutes after you'd left, because I couldn't get away from the job I was doing till the last minute and then I got caught up in a big traffic jam.'

'Oh!'

Tessa was conscious of a warm feeling inside her. Suddenly the world seemed a much nicer place. He'd gone to the airport and now he was here. He wanted to see her!

'You were nearly late for the tapas,' Manuel said with mock reproach. 'I will go and fetch them now.' He smiled conspiratorially at Tessa. 'And now you will find out about the children.'

He vanished into the kitchen. They could hear his voice raised though they could not grasp the words, but suddenly the kitchen door burst open as Maria and Juan hurtled though it. Tessa just had time to push back her chair and stand up before they threw their arms round her and Tom, enveloping them in their embraces.

'Tessa! Tom! Nuestros amigos!'

Behind them came Joaquin himself, and following him came Manuel's daughter, Sofia, her pleasant, homely face also smiling a welcome. Tessa found herself at the centre of a lot of kisses and hugs until finally Sofia shooed the children and their father back into the kitchen.

'Now you eat in peace,' she said firmly.

Tom and Tessa sat down, laughing. The children's appearance had helped them relax.

'So the little family is still here,' marvelled Diane. 'What happened?'

Tom shrugged.

'Luck, to start with. Manuel's assistant decided to stay with her father in Madrid, so Joaquin and the children have been able to remain here, and he's been working for me as well when I need help.'

'And what came after luck?' enquired Tessa.

'More luck, I suppose. Sofia has decided that he is the man for her, and she is a very determined young lady.'

The two girls gasped.

'And how does Joaquin feel about it?' Diane demanded.

'He appears perfectly happy about it. She and the children get on well so there is no problem there, and Manuel is looking forward to lots of grandchildren.'

Tessa gave a gusty sigh.

'I'm so glad it's worked out well!' She turned to Tom. 'I'll never forget looking for them in the woods in that rainstorm.'

Tom nodded.

'And the relief we felt when we found them on the doorstep!'

Those memories brought back other shared memories and Tessa reddened and looked down, avoiding his eyes, searching for something else to talk about.

'The hotel manager was telling me how Valdes seemed more afraid of his father than the police.'

'And with good reason! His father did not want the police checking on what Pedro Valdes had been doing for his business, but they did and found that the business had criminal links with some very nasty characters. Pedro Valdes himself had been threatened with violence when he got things wrong and I've heard that his father appears to have left Spain for South America.'

Manuel and Sofia were bustling

cheerfully round them, Diane and Matt were glowing with happiness, and it was impossible not to enjoy the evening. Coffee and brandy rounded off the meal as usual. Matt insisted on paying for everyone.

'I asked you to come. You are my guests,' he announced. 'Besides, after my recent business trip and the contract I signed, I can afford it.'

Matt was ready to walk back to the hotel with the two girls, and Tom said he would go with them.

'You and Diane go ahead,' he told Matt. 'I want a word with Tessa.'

What word? Was he going to tell her after all that getting in touch with him had been a mistake and he didn't want to have any more to do with her? Tessa felt suddenly apprehensive. Tom was watching the other pair walk away, hand in hand.

'It looks like a happy ending for them, anyway. I'll order us another coffee,' he said. 'I must talk to you, and those two won't notice that we're not following them.'

Manuel brought the coffee and then, as if at some signal, he and Sofia left the two of them alone. Tom stirred his coffee, put down his spoon, and then picked it up and started stirring it again, his attention apparently focussed on the cup as if it was the most important thing in the world. Finally, just as she felt ready to lean over and snatch the spoon from him, he stopped stirring and looked at Tessa.

'First of all, I want to apologise for my behaviour that last night at the hotel. My only excuse is that I did want you very much, and I thought I would never see you again after that night. As it is, I've spent the weeks since you left thinking what a selfish animal I must have seemed, and how right you were to send me away.'

'I wasn't exactly repulsing you until that last moment,' Tessa said quietly. 'And for many couples a one-night stand is just something to enjoy.'

'But it wasn't for you.'

'At the last moment, no. I decided it wasn't enough for me.'

Tom gave a kind of laugh.

'I understand. Sleeping together means commitment to you, and you made it clear from the first time I met you that you didn't want a man like me or a life style like mine.'

Tessa realised that she was gripping her hands together so tightly that it hurt.

'I may have over-stated that a bit,' she said carefully, and then looked full into his eyes. 'But, remember, you also made it very clear that I wasn't the type of woman you were looking for — that you wanted the outdoor, capable type — not someone who went for a walk in unsuitable shoes and couldn't even recognise half the trees you've got.'

'What I got was a woman who was prepared to face a storm to rescue a stranger's children, who cared for them tenderly, who was supposed to be on holiday and yet was prepared to spend hours dragging round back streets to

306

try to find their father. Still, it's too late now. You've gone back to the life you like and can forget about me. I'm just glad that I had this chance to say that I'm sorry.'

Tessa leant forward. His left hand was resting on the top of the table and she laid her hand over it, feeling it warm beneath her touch.

'Too late for what?' she asked.

The silence seemed to drag on.

'Too late to say that I love you,' Tom said so quietly that she could hardly hear the words.

'What?'

'I love you.'

This time his voice was clear and distinct. A couple at another table looked over at them and smiled. Tessa threw her napkin down on the table.

'Let's get out of here. We can talk as we walk by the sea.'

They stood up and made for the door, which Manuel hurried to open for them.

'Good night, my friends,' he said,

beaming fondly at them.

Tessa managed a smile in return.

'Good night, Manuel. It was a lovely evening.'

Then she and Tom walked out into the starlit night. They strolled along without speaking or even looking at each other till they came to a low wall. Tom leant on it, looking out over the sea.

'Tessa, I mean it when I say I love you, but I'm not a hopeless romantic. I know that it doesn't follow that you are compelled to fall in love with me in return, and I'm not going to try to make you.' He fell silent while Tessa struggled to find the words she needed. Before she had found them he spoke again. 'There is one thing that's been puzzling me. Why did you send me that email? Obviously, you wanted Matt to know that Diane was coming, but why me, when you'd made it so clear what you thought of me? I came to the airport to see you because I assumed you wanted to find out what had happened to Joaquin and his children. Was that right, or did you think we might see each other by accident so you wanted to warn me to keep away?'

Tessa finally knew what she had to say.

'I sent it to you because I wanted to see you again. Over the past few weeks I have found that the life I have in England is not enough. I didn't know what I wanted instead, though, until something made me realise that what I want is you.' She faced him. 'It's true that we have spent very little time together, but we spent it in circumstances that have shown us our true selves. It's too soon to say that we could be happy together for ever — our lives have been very different and we'd need to adapt to each other — but I think we should try to find out if we are suited. You would have to give up your independence, your liberty, and that might be too much to ask. I'd have to forget about indoor bathrooms and convenient shops and a lot of comforts

I've always taken for granted. But you say you love me, so are you willing to explore the possibility that we might be meant for each other? I know I am.'

She waited for his reply, but instead she found herself in his arms, held tight against his heart.

She smelt the tang of fresh sweat, caught an echo of the fragrance of the fruit trees, felt the strong warmth of his body. This was where she belonged. This was home.

THE END

We do hope that you have enjoyed reading this large print book.

Did you know that all of our titles are available for purchase?

We publish a wide range of high quality large print books including:
Romances, Mysteries, Classics
General Fiction
Non Fiction and Westerns

Special interest titles available in large print are:
The Little Oxford Dictionary
Music Book, Song Book
Hymn Book, Service Book

Also available from us courtesy of Oxford University Press:
Young Readers' Dictionary
(large print edition)
Young Readers' Thesaurus
(large print edition)

For further information or a free brochure, please contact us at:
Ulverscroft Large Print Books Ltd.,
The Green, Bradgate Road, Anstey,
Leicester, LE7 7FU, England.
Tel: (00 44) **0116 236 4325**
Fax: (00 44) **0116 234 0205**

Other titles in the
Linford Romance Library:

YOUR SECRET SMILE

Suzanne Ross Jones

When Sean left town to go travelling, he took a piece of Grace's heart with him. It's taken years for her to get over him and at last she's reached a place where she's happy on her own. Her time is filled with good friends and fulfilling work as a maths teacher. But when Sean reappears as an art teacher at Grace's school, it's obvious he's intent on causing havoc in her well-ordered life.

ACCIDENT PRONE

Anna Ramsay

From hospital ward sister to sanatorium sister at Ditchingham Prep School is a drastic change, but Ruth Silke needs something different. Working with Dr Daniel Gather, the local GP who covers the school, isn't so easy — particularly when he seems all too matter-of-fact about his young son Danny, a boarder at the school. Ruth is convinced that Danny's accidents are a cry for help, but how to persuade Dan? Particularly when their own relationship leaves so much to be desired . . .

FAIR FLOWER OF NORTHUMBERLAND

Harriet Smith

Amanda believes that Justin is cold-bloodedly planning to marry her step-sister for her money. She allows him only one good quality: he is clever, especially at putting her in the wrong. When she is forced to revise her opinion, she admits that she judged too hastily — but the last thing she expected was to find herself fathoms deep in love with the object of her distrust . . .